Loyal to the Game 3

T.J. & Jelissa

Lock Down Publications & Ca$h Presents
Loyal to the Game 3

.

T.J. & Jelissa

Lock Down Publications
P.O. Box 1482
Pine Lake, Ga 30072-1482

Visit our website at **www.lockdownpublications.com**

First Edition August 2017
Printed in the United States of America
This is a work of fiction. Names, characters, places, and incidents either are products of the author's imagination or are used fictitiously. Any similarity to actual events or locales or persons, living or dead, is entirely coincidental.

Cover design and layout by: Dynasty's Cover Me
Book interior design by: Shawn Walker
Edited by: Lauren Burton

Stay Connected with Us!

Text **LOCKDOWN** to 22828 to stay up-to-date with new releases, sneak peaks, contests and more…

Thank you!

Submission Guideline.

Submit the first three chapters of your completed manuscript to ldpsubmissions@gmail.com, subject line: Your book's title. The manuscript must be in a .doc file and sent as an attachment. Document should be in Times New Roman, double spaced and in size 12 font. Also, provide your synopsis and full contact information. If sending multiple submissions, they must each be in a separate email.

Have a story but no way to send it electronically? You can still submit to LDP/Ca$h Presents. Send in the first three chapters, written or typed, of your completed manuscript to:

LDP: Submissions Dept
Po Box 1482
Pine Lake, Ga 30072

DO NOT send original manuscript. Must be a duplicate.

Provide your synopsis and a cover letter containing your full contact information.

Thanks for considering LDP and Ca$h Presents.

DEDICATION

First and foremost, we give our thanks to the Lord above because without Him none of this would be possible. We wouldn't be who we are without Him.

This book is dedicated to our two little men, Rae'Jon and A'Jhani. All that we do, we do for you two.

To our mother, Deborah Lynn Edwards, who is always in our hearts, may you always rest in peace.

T.J. & Jelissa

Chapter 1

Tiny

I read over the short note again and tried my best to keep from screaming. There I was, not even five minutes into freedom, and my heart was already being ripped in two. I mean, I had not even had the chance to make it home before the dark angel of pain called my number. I sat there in the middle of the parking lot, rocking back and forth with tears streaming down my face.

Once again, I reread the note. The contents read:

Welcome home, Zivial. We have a lot of unfinished business. You owe me, an eye for an eye. Alexis being returned to you comes with a price. I'll be in touch. Oh, and it's true what they say. Chocolate does melt in your mouth.

Signed,
an old friend

That's what kept on getting the better of me, the whole part where this person was trying to insinuate they were doing something of a sexual nature to my daughter. That was the part that had me on the verge of having a nervous breakdown.

Alexis was my seventeen-year-old daughter, and she was the love of my life. There was nothing I would not do for her or about her.

I had served nearly 18 years in prison for a crime I did not commit, all because some broad thought it was in her best interest to try to attack me over what I had going on with her perverted-ass father. She tried to kill me with a knife after surprising me in my own apartment, and in my haste to get away from her, I knocked over a chair to create some distance in between us while I made a run for the door. This chick wound up tripping over it while holding the knife in her hand, and unfortunately when she fell the knife wound up going inside of her and taking her life. So if you asked me my opinion, I would say she committed suicide by ignorance. Because of her ignorance, I had lost the majority of my life, and I had been locked away so far for all of my daughter's life.

Alexis was raised within the foster system after my parents released her into it. I had met her physically for the first time when she was already 16 years old.

This was my first day of freedom, and there was no one I wanted to see more than her, yet out of everyone in my life I cared for, she was the only one not present, and it was breaking my heart.

I wondered who it was that had my baby. The note said it was an *old friend*. I knew that was the person's way of being cute. I knew 'old friend' actually meant an old enemy. Was it Chris, the man whom I still owed $70,000? The same man who had taken me and Alexis' father hostage, putting guns to our mouths all because Avery had vouched for a dude who wound up being a thief?

Or was it somebody from Lisa's family? It wasn't my fault her clumsy-ass fell and wound up killing herself. She shouldn't have been in my apartment that day, trying to come for me. What happened between her nasty-ass father and I had nothing to do with her. His ass should've been the one dead. I didn't have many enemies because for the most part I tried to do right by everybody. I had a very good heart, and that was actually my weakness. I didn't know who had my baby, but I was going to find out, and when I did, all bets were off. Never mess with a woman's child, especially when she is the ultimate Momma Lion.

Roman, my cousin, came over and placed his arm around my shoulder. He was kneeling down beside me just as rain began to fall down from the sky. There was a quick flash of lightning, followed by a loud, thunderous boom. I felt him pulling me up along with the rest of the people who had come to see me step into freedom after 18 years of confinement. The rain began coming down so hard it felt like each drop was slamming into my face out of anger, yet I did not want to move.

"Get up, Tiny. Come on, and let me get you into the car. I know you're spacing right now, but we're going to figure this whole thing out together," he said before picking me up forcefully and tossing me onto his shoulder.

Ariana, my goddaughter, ran ahead and opened the passenger door to his Range Rover. "Come on, Roman, get her in there before she gets sick. That's my mother, and I love her. Please don't allow anything to happen to her," she said, with the rain bouncing off of her high-yellow face.

Ariana was the biological daughter of one of my friends I used to sell pussy with. We had the same pimp, and in a sense the same baby's father, though I had failed to bring my child to term because our Pimp, Jaheim, had beaten it out of me within its early stages of development.

Her mother's name was Amber, and Amber had committed suicide after battling drug addiction and severe depression. She knew she would not ever be able to be a mother to Ariana, and that caused her to go into a deep depression and she slit both of her wrists while she was in Rehab. I had been by Ariana's side before we even knew she would make it. She was born addicted to heroin and crack cocaine, and extremely premature. But, she'd pulled through and had become one of the most beautiful women I had ever seen in my life. I loved her as if she were my own.

No one would ever be able to tell me this child was not mine.

I allowed Roman to get me into the truck and drape a seatbelt across me. The water on my forehead trickled down my face, feeling as though something was crawling on me. I slapped my hand to my face so fast I poked myself in the eye. I hollered out in pain. "Fuck! This is just not my day!" I began slamming my fists onto my thighs and kicking my legs. "Where is my daughter? Where is Alexis? I need to see my baby. I need my little girl!" I had my hands over my face, bawling like a two-year-old child.

Roman leaned over and hugged me tight. "Look, Tiny, you already know we about to get her back. All you gotta do is maintain your composure. Let's get you to the house, get some food in you, then we gon' look at this thing logically." He kissed me on the forehead and tightened his hug. "You hear me?"

I nodded my head as tears of pain flowed down my cheeks, hitting my shirt like darts. There was no way I was eating anything. I did not have an appetite. All I could think about was somebody putting their filthy hands all over my pure daughter, and the fact it was my fault. She did not deserve whatever was happening to her. Once again my sins had caught up to her, and she bore my punishment.

Ariana reached over the seat and rubbed my shoulder, squeezing it. "Mom, if it makes you feel any better, I love you and believe in you. And I know you're going to get my sister back because you are our hero. Until she is back, I'm going to love you like crazy for the both of us." That did make me feel somewhat better. I mean, I could not lose sight of the fact Ariana also needed me and I was no longer behind prison walls. Had I gotten this note just yesterday, I would have lost my mind because there would have been no way I could have done anything about her ransom. But here I was, no longer bound by the bars that had held me captive for 18 years. I knew whatever it took, no matter what that was, I was going to make shit happen.

***

I sat at the kitchen table at Roman's house, rolling my neck around on my shoulders while Ariana rubbed my back, kissing me on the cheek sporadically. She took my hair out of my face and smiled at me. I had a glass of orange juice I was sipping. I was trying to get something into my stomach because I was starting to feel dizzy. I had already taken two Aspirin.

Roman came into the kitchen with his shirt off, and it looked like he was flexing. He had muscles on top of muscles, even up and down his stomach. He had so many tattoos it looked like he had been drawn on by a whole kindergarten class. He stood in front of me, and slowly Ariana went from rubbing my back to kneeling down on the side of me, looking up at him as if he were her last meal, licking her lips and making faint moaning noises I didn't think she was aware she was making.

"So, what you wanna do, cuz? I'm down for whatever you thinking will be necessary." He grabbed my glass from me and trailed his thumb across my forehead, then cupped my face. I could smell his cologne. "You know I got you, right? I mean, you know we about to make it happen for her, don't you?"

I nodded my head, turned my head to the side, and kissed the palm of his hand, grabbing it and wrapping my smaller hand into his. "Yeah, I know. I'm just ready for the next instructions. I'm just ready to get her back, Roman. That's all." I sniffed quietly, tears threatening to spill from my eyes.

Jackie came into the room with shorts on so small I could clearly make out her sex lips. I mean, those white boy shorts were hugging her like a second skin. I scrunched my face at the caramel-colored, pretty-faced girl. "So, who are you to my daughter, again?" I asked, looking down at her ample ass, as she reached into the refrigerator and came out with bottled water. The boy shorts had literally hid themselves within the crack of her ass. I mean, both butt cheeks were out so much I could make out the faint hints of stretch marks along them. They couldn't help but jiggle every time she barely moved.

"I lived at the Taylor Foster House with your daughter for nearly five years. She was like a sister to me. I am the one who helped us get away from those people. I'm so sorry, Ms. Johnson. I am willing to help out in any way that I can, you have my word on that," she said, coming over and kissing me on the forehead.

"Thank you, baby. That means a lot to me." I smiled at her after looking her over from head to toe once again. That li'l girl was stacked. Even I was having a hard time

14

not catching a hard on, and I didn't even have a penis. Her body was something to see. I mean, I had seen a lot of forms of the female body, but this girl's was incredible.

"Yeah, and I'm here for you, too," a slim, white girl said, walking into the kitchen and flipping her long hair over her left shoulder. "My name is Leah, and your daughter and I are best friends. We were roommates at the Taylor House for over three years. We absolutely know everything that there is to know about each other, and there isn't anything I wouldn't do for her, or for you. I mean that from the bottom of my heart. I need to help."

She gave me a begging look that said she was beyond serious. She also knelt down in front of me in a total submission-like fashion, looking up into my eyes and giving me the chance to zoom into her own, which were the lightest shade of blue. She was an extremely attractive female with two deep dimples on each side of her cheeks, and just above her lip, slightly to the right, was a little mole.

"Thank you, baby, and I can tell you really care about her. As soon as I figure some things out, I will surely let you know how it is you can help out. So don't worry, you will have a place in all of this." I leaned down and kissed her on the forehead.

She shuddered at my touch, and then looked up at me and smiled shyly. "I. Wow. You are even more beautiful in person than Alexis let on," she said, looking at me as if she couldn't believe I was real.

I smiled and rubbed her cheek with my thumb. There was the sound of loud sirens going off outside somewhere, and I estimated it had to be about four blocks over. The rain continued to come down and beat against the house while loud thunder roared somewhere in the heavens.

Ariana walked up to Roman and wrapped her arms around him while he rubbed her back. "I just want us to find my sister, Roman. I want us to bring her home safely so she can be with us and we can all be one big family. I feel so empty without her being here with us right now." She laid her head on to his chest and sighed.

"I just need everybody to chill. We need to take this night and get our minds together. Tomorrow, after we get a good night's sleep, we'll all come together around the table and decide what we're going to do to bring my li'l cousin back home." He squeezed her tighter, then Jackie came over and they both hugged him.

I watched as he wrapped his arm around her waist and pulled her to him possessively. Her ass cheeks jiggled as she crashed into him and caught her balance.

I yawned and stood up. "Alright, that sounds like a nice plan. Clearly we aren't going to get anything accomplished here tonight, especially with my mind being all over the place."

Leah stood up and wrapped her arm around my neck. "Come on, Ms. Johnson, let me walk you to the guest room where you can relax and get your mind together."

I allowed her to walk me up the steps and down the hall, into the bedroom where I sat on the big bed paralyzed. She came over to me and knelt at my foot. She reached and took first one of my shoes off, and then the other one. Then she took off my socks and proceeded to give me a firm foot rub.

Even though what she was doing had taken me off guard, I had to admit it felt awesome, and I was beginning to relax a little bit. I was trying to wrap my head around the fact my daughter was missing and I didn't know the first step to getting her back. Every ounce of my being wanted to shut down, and I wanted to scream and cry until I ran out of bodily fluids, but I knew it wouldn't help matters any. The bottom line was there would be nothing I or any of us could do until we heard back from her captors.

Leah continued to rub my feet and pull on my little toes. She balled up her fist and massaged the bottom of my left foot, making me purr out loud.

"Do you like that, Ms. Johnson, or would you like for me to be a little softer?" she asked, looking up to me, concerned.

I closed my eyes. "Baby, what you're doing is perfect. Just don't stop. The only thing I want you to stop doing is calling me Ms. Johnson. You don't have to call me that," I said, lying back on the bed.

"Can I call you Mom? Oh my god, that would be so cool. Then I could be like your daughter, and you could be like the mother I never really had. I mean, I had one, but she gave me up because she didn't care about me anymore. But you still love Alexis after all of these years, and that's just so cool because you're so beautiful and kind, and I would just love if I could call you Mom."

She said all of these words so fast I could barely keep up. "It's okay, baby. You can call me mom. I would love it if you did that. In fact, I would be honored." I smiled with my eyes closed. I felt she had stopped rubbing my feet, and that caused me to look down to check on her.

Leah sat holding my feet in her hands, crying real tears. She started to rub my feet again before holding the left foot up and kissing my toes. She actually kissed each one individually, then picked up my right foot and did the

same. "I will worship and cherish you, Mom. You're so cool. I can't believe you see me as your daughter already. That means the world to me.
I will never let you down, or at least I will try not to."

She began kissing my toes all over again and rubbing them across her lips. I didn't know what was going on inside of this little girl's mind, but clearly she was going through something. I didn't want to interrupt her in any way. Besides, all the kisses felt good, so I let her continue on doing what she was doing.

Before it was all said and done, she had rubbed my toes all over her face and her shockingly thick lips. She kept on saying she loved me and she would worship me, and even though I didn't know her like that, something in me truly believed she was telling the truth.

Chapter 2

Ariana

I know my sister was missing, but I could not help the throbbing from inside of my kitty. My clitoris was vibrating so much I couldn't do anything but squeeze my thighs together and stuff my pillow more firmly between my legs. Why did Roman have to walk around with his shirt off? That always drove me crazy, and it made me have visions of him snatching me up and raping me the way I needed to be. I needed him to just take advantage of me. To throw me against the wall, pick me up, and stuff his big dick all the way inside of my little hole. I needed that grown man meat. I wanted to suck his dick so I could show him I knew what I was doing.

I spread my legs wide and humped upward into my pillow, making sure the edge of the pillow went right up my vagina's crease. I smashed it into me so I could feel all of the pressure on my clitty. I couldn't help moaning a little bit when I felt that spark shoot through me, causing my nipples to stand up like it was freezing cold in the room. And I have really huge nipples, too. They stand out almost an inch when I am fully aroused. I love having them pulled on and sucked so hard it makes me scream. Damn, I needed Roman's dick.

I peeked across the dark room to see if Jackie was awake or if she was sound asleep. I held my breath to see if I could hear her breathing regularly. After I confirmed she indeed was, I spread my legs farther and kicked the sheets off of me. I took two fingers on my right hand and rubbed my panties into my sex lips, loving the feel of the soft satin against my pearl. It felt so good I could not stop moaning. "Fuck, I'm horny. I need somebody to touch me down there. Somebody has to take advantage of me, please," I whimpered out loud.

I pulled my panties to the side aggressively, pried my sex lips apart, and rammed two fingers inside of myself, making me jerk up from the bed. I tore my shirt trying to get to my breast, squeezing it and trapping the nipple between my thumb and forefinger, pinching it so hard I started crying and finger-fucked myself even faster.

I imagined Roman raping me and forcing me to be his bitch. I wanted him to use me and treat me like a little mixed whore. I wanted him to fuck me until my pussy was raw and dry from being sexed up.

"Mm, yes, take this pussy, Roman. Take this pussy, daddy. Please rape me. Please! I need you to take this shit!" I hollered, unable to control myself.

You know what? Fuck this. Fuck this shit. I got up out of the bed and walked over to Jackie with my fingers still deep inside of me. I stood over her for a moment before tapping her on the shoulder.

She roused with a stir, squinting her eyes in an attempt to see me clearly. "What's up, Ariana? Hey, what's the matter?" She tried to sit up in the bed, but her headphones fell off of her lap and crashed to the floor. She leaned down to pick them up, and that's when I noted she had fallen asleep without a bra on. Her breasts were firm and juicy, the nipples black as a blackberry.

I took two steps to my left and closed our bedroom door and locked it. I walked back over to her and knelt down by her bed while she looked at me like I was crazy or my head was on backwards or something. I didn't care how she was looking at me. I was ready to take her pussy. I needed her to either fuck me with something, or to fuck me with her fingers until I came all over the palm of her hand. Either way, I needed some relief.

"Ariana, what's the problem? Why are you looking at me like a lunatic, and what are you doing knelt beside my bed?" she asked with a voice that sounded heavy with sleep.

"Jackie, I need you to fuck me real hard and real fast. Please. My pussy is throbbing, and I need something in my little hole or I am going to go crazy." I reached and rubbed her stomach over the blanket. It felt so firm, and she smelled so damn good. I needed her black pussy rubbing against mine, and I needed it now. I slid my hand under her blanket and squeezed her breast before pulling on her long, erect nipple.

She jerked up from the bed. "Holy shit, Ariana, what are you doing?" Though she asked this question, she did not stop me from trailing my hand downward until I was at the top of her thighs. I pinched them, and she spread them wide, giving me all access.

As soon as they opened up, I felt the heat radiate from her cave. I slid my hand down and cupped her entire pussy, spreading her lips with my two fingers. At the same time, I slid my middle finger deep within her. She jerked up from the bed again and moaned my name. I slid another finger inside of her and felt her womb gripping them hungrily. I knew I was about to turn this broad out.

My foster mother had done more than enough numbers on me. I knew how to make a girl come so much she would pass out. At that moment, that wasn't on my mind. All I cared about was the fire between my own legs. I just needed this bitch to extinguish it for me.

"Listen to me, Jackie, and I'm not playing with you," I said, finger-fucking her so hard my wrist was slamming into her ass. "I want you to get out of this bed and lay on top of me, and put three fingers into me and fuck me as hard as you possibly can. You have to tell me I'm a ho, tell me you're taking my pussy and I belong to you. Do you got that?" I asked, leaning over and sucking her clitoris into my mouth, while my fingers went in and out of her at full speed.

"Yes! Yes. Oh fuck, yes. I hear you. I hear you loud and clear. Please don't stop. I'll do anything, just don't stop! Please!" she hollered, humping into my assaulting fingers until I felt her tense up, clamp her legs around my hand, and start shaking like she was having a seizure. "Aw, yes! Yes! Oh, shit!"

She grabbed me and pulled me by the hair until my lips were pressed against hers. Once there, I bit her lip until I tasted blood. I then dragged her out of the bed and laid her on the floor, got on top of her, positioning our kittens against each other, and ground her for all she was worth. I held my sex lips apart to get a better feel, biting my bottom lip and squeezed her juicy, perfect titties.

She held my waist, slid her hands down, and grabbed ahold of my ass, making me hump her even harder. Our pussies were dripping wet, and the scent in the room was all feminine.

When I felt her reach down for my womanhood, I flipped onto my back and held my legs wide open. "Don't play with my pussy, Jackie. If you're going to fuck me, then you make sure you hurt me real good. Give me them fingers, please! Please, just give them to me already, bitch!"

"Bitch?" She pushed one of my knees to my chest, opening me up as wide as possible, and slammed her fingers into me hard. "I'm a bitch, huh? You wanna call me out of my name, bitch, I'm about to injure your shit," Jackie said, fucking me so hard I wanted to marry her ass.

This was the same treatment my foster mother gave me at her house, in her bedroom when her husband left for work. I mean, she never even waited until he was out of the driveway before she was all over me, forcing me to eat her roughly while she pulled on my nipples and told me how much trash I really was. She would then push my knees to my chest and fuck me with her toy until I came and came, then she would make me eat her stanky pussy.

Jackie sucked on my pearl while she jammed three fingers in and out of me. She was doing magic on my vagina's button. I couldn't believe how much she had me squirming all over the floor like a tramp in heat. The harder she fucked me, the more I felt myself emotionally falling for her.

***

Tiny

I woke up with Leah snuggled all under me. She had her leg around my waist and her arm draped across my chest. I felt a little awkward, but not so much so that I wanted to push her small, white ass on the floor. I just came to the conclusion she needed a mother, and the relationship she'd had with my daughter had caused her to feel some type of way about me, which was cool. She had spent the entire night worshipping my toes and kissing my feet, telling me over and over again I was her Queen, and she honored me as such.

Ariana swung open the door and burst into the room in a frenzy. "Mom! Mom, look! I got a message from Alexis. She's Facetiming me."

She tried to get over to me so fast she tripped and fell, landing on the side of the bed. From the floor she tossed the phone onto the bed. I picked it up and saw my daughter's face. I nearly fainted.

"Alexis? Alexis, baby, can you hear me? Please tell me you're okay?" I whined, trying my best to work the phone. I zoomed into the screen and saw she had tears all over her chocolate face. I wished I could have jumped into the phone in that moment and saved my baby girl. Seeing her tears was enough to break my heart in half. I felt like I was having a heart attack.

"Mom? Mom, is that you?" she asked, looking into the phone. Her voice constantly broke up, and I could not tell where she was, yet I could make out someone was standing behind her in all black with a handful of her hair.

"Yes, baby, it's me. Your mother is right here. Please know I have been going crazy looking for you. I love you, Alexis. If nothing more, I need for you to know that, because you are my life." I was already crying real tears, sobbing and everything.

"Mom, they got me, and they aren't going to let me go until we pay them $500,000. I don't know what we're going to do, or where we're going to get the money from, but you have to save me. Please, Mommy? Please save your little girl."

Her head jerked backward and the camera pointed toward the ceiling. A man put his face into the camera, so close it caused his image to become distorted. It took him a while to feel the camera feed out, but when he did, I was able to identify him clearly. I nearly fell off the bed. My eyes got so big they hurt.

"What's the matter, Tiny? Bitch, you acting like you done seen a ghost," Jaheim said, laughing at the top of his lungs. "Oh, what, you thought everything we had going on in the past was just about to fade away because yo' punk ass got locked up? Bitch, please!"

He laughed out loud again, then in a snap his face was frowning. He looked directly into the camera and snarled, "Bitch, you take my top money-making white bitch from me while she's pregnant, mentally manipulate the bitch so bad until she killed herself, just so yo' trifling ass could steal our kid?" He turned to the side and spit out a loogie. "You see, bitch, you have always been obsessed with me every since I could remember, but I never thought you would stoop so muthafucking low. I can't wait to put a bullet right in the middle of your forehead. Bitch so dirty she took my firstborn daughter away. Now, ain't that a bitch?" He spit again, and this time wiped his mouth.

I was starting to shake all over as if I was sitting ass-naked in the snow. I could not believe this man had my daughter, and I could also not believe he had held a grudge for nearly 18 years, a grudge for things I didn't even do. I mean, not one thing he named I had actually done.

"Jaheim, all of these things you are saying I did are false. They just aren't true. Amber killed herself because she was too strung out on narcotics that you got her hooked on. She said she would not be able to care for Ariana, and that made her feel like the worst failure in the world. The night prior to her killing herself, I did all I could to save her, to put her in a different state of mind, but those drugs had her gone, and she did not have a handle on them. After she passed away, I vowed I would never allow Ariana to be lost to the streets like we were. I promised to make sure she had a home to go to and a mother. I never took her away from you. We just never knew where you were." Quiet as I kept, I would have never allowed her to be a part of him in any way because he was extremely trifling. On top of that, I had very little power over Ariana during this time because I was locked down.

"Bitch, who you think you running that drag too? Don't forget, I'm the one that taught your yellow ass how to lie, so I know when you're trying to con me." He grabbed Alexis by the neck and licked her from the chin all the way up to her forehead, only stopping to grab a handful of her hair. "But you know what? Your li'l bitch so bad I'm pretty sure it was a nice and even trade. Look at this! I mean, let me make her stand up." He grabbed her upward by her hair. "Stand up, bitch, so I can show your momma how fine yo' li'l ass done got since she been gone," he said, yanking her out of the chair.

She jolted to her feet, almost falling over. The sight of that made me cry even harder. He turned her so her backside was facing the camera, then I watched as he pawed his hands all over her, even sliding them under and in between her legs. I watched as they disappeared, and then Alexis yelped.

"You see what I'm talking about?" he laughed. "My li'l bitch can't be as bad as this one because she's half white. Being half white don't get you all of this ass. This that shit that's straight from the bloodline of the motherland, pure and uncut." He forced his hand upward, and Alexis stood on her tippy-toes and groaned in what sounded like pain.

26

"You sick son of a bitch! You let my daughter go. You let her go! She's just a little girl, and she didn't do nothing to your trifling ass!" I screamed at the top of my lungs, falling off of the bed and landing on an open pizza box. A few slices of pizza stuck to my hand and wrist. I could feel the cheese and sauce ooze through my fingers, but I didn't care. I got up and grabbed the phone out of Leah's hands just in time to see him tearing Alexis' shirt off of her, leaving her standing in just her bra.

"Oh, what's the matter? Did somebody not take anger management when they were locked down?" He put his face into the camera and poked his bottom lip out. " Po' baby. Aw, daddy so sorry. But not sorry." He looked directly into the camera lens and growled, "Listen here, bitch, I'm not about to keep playing with you. The fee is $500,000 for this li'l chocolate bitch. That's the price you owe me for over 18 years of interest. I'm not accepting a penny less than that. Have my shit in two weeks, or I promise you I'm gon' make this li'l bitch fuck until she literally die." He yanked her head backward and cupped her mound in the front. "Now, don't get it twisted. I'm about to fuck her right now. Ain't no way in hell I'm about to let this piece of pussy pass me by. I remember when you and I first got together, Tiny. You had a nice li'l shot on you. After working night after night, that pussy started to get too many miles on it. I didn't even like you touching me after a while, but in the beginning that pussy was good," he said, opening the front of Alexis' pants and sliding his hand down the front of them, making her groan out.

She stood on her tippy toes while he dug further into them. It was almost unbearable to watch.

"Jaheim, okay, look. Just leave her alone. I'll get your money, I'll get every red cent you're asking for. Just please leave my baby alone. Please, I am asking you to have mercy on her, please, because she has nothing to do with you and I." I fell to my knees with the phone. I was losing my fight and my will to handle this situation in general. Nobody should ever have to watch their little girl go through what she was going through.

She yelped again and stood all the way up on the tips of her toes as if she were a ballerina.

"Yo, and this li'l minx is a virgin. Aw shit, I'm about to play with this. Everybody knows it ain't nothing like some fresh-ass pussy." His hand began moving in her unzipped pants before he took them out and sucked his fingers in front of the camera. "Tasty li'l Hershey right there, and that's crazy because I usually like a li'l Milkyway." He laughed and slid his hand back into her pants.

"This how this shit gon' work. I'm gon' hit you up in thirteen days inquiring about my money, and when I do, your only answer better be that you'll have it in the morning. If not, I'm gon' make this bitch fuck 30 niggas over and over again until she pass out. When that happens, I'm gon' cut this bitch up and mail her to you. You took my daughter, now I'm gon' make you pay to get yours back. You got that?" He licked Alexis' face and kissed her on the cheek. "I got your numbers. I'll hit you up when the time is right. Otherwise, bye, Felicia!"

The phone went blank, and so did my mind. I dropped the phone and started to bawl my eyes out.

Chapter 3

Tiny

I couldn't sleep that night. My daughter was on my mind like crazy; I mean, worse than ever before. I had already cried myself out of tears. I cried so much I literally ran out of fluids. I tried to take a piss and it hurt so bad I just stood and pulled my panties up because I couldn't.

I didn't know how I was going to get $500,000, and neither did anybody in the house. I couldn't even leave the bedroom because every time I tried to, I felt woozy. I knew I was on the clock, but I didn't even know where to begin.

Leah stayed by my feet the whole time, rubbing and kissing them. I didn't know what was going through her mind.

The whole house was full of silence. Roman came and knocked on the bedroom door early in the morning. He entered, leaned down, and gave me a kiss on the forehead. "Look, cuz, I know you sick as hell right now, but you gotta eat. Why don't you come on down to breakfast so you can put something in your stomach?" he asked, rubbing my back.

I gave him a look that told him I was not in the mood to eat anything right then or anytime soon. In fact, food was the furthest thing from my mind. I had to find a way to get my baby out of the jam she was in. There was no way in hell I, as a mother, could sit back and allow my child to be tortured while I sat at some breakfast table feasting on fried eggs and grits, or whatever he'd made for me. That was not an option for me.

He sighed and then took a step backward. "Okay, I can see that's not going to happen. Well, sooner or later you're going to have to eat something, it is impossible to think on your toes when you haven't given any fuel to your body." He rubbed my chin, and kissed my forehead. "We'll figure this whole thing out, just trust and believe that we will."

I started to get a little angry. I didn't know why I was getting angry at him, but the fact of the matter was I really was. For some unexplained reason, his voice was starting to drive me nuts. I just got so tired of him telling me that everything was going to be okay without offering me a solution. How in the hell was everything going to be okay when we only had 13 days before my daughter was killed? Jaheim wanted $500,000, and I didn't even have a thousand dollars to my name. The more he tried to console me, the more I wanted to get up and punch him right in his handsome face.

"Why are you looking at me like that?" he asked, turning his head to the side as if he were a dog or something.

"To be honest with you, Roman, I just need for you to shut up and get out of my face with all of your irritating-ass optimism. You got all this fucking positive energy with no solution, and it's starting to make me want to kick your extra muscle-bound ass. I'm not bullshitting, either." I frowned, ready to jump up out of my bed. In that moment I hated every man on the face of the earth, anything with a penis. I wanted to kill for what was transpiring with my daughter, and it just so happened that Roman had a penis, and I hated him because of it.

He shook his head and lowered it to the floor. "Damn. So, what? I'm the enemy now?" He rubbed his earlobe, then ran the palm of his hand over the top of his head.

I stood up out of the bed and got into his face, it didn't help that my period had come in the middle of that night, so I was extra irritated. I poked him in the chest. "I should have never left your stupid-ass in charge of Alexis. You wasn't even there to protect my daughter. She wasn't with you for one week before she was abducted!" I spat, bumping my chest against his in a vain attempt to move him a few inches.

He looked down on me and made the saddest face I had ever seen in my life. "You know what, cousin? You're right, and I been thinking about that every single day. I don't know how I am going to get this money for her, but I am, because you are right."

He started to make his way out of the room, but I ran in front of him and blocked his path.

"Move, Tiny, for real, because I'm not in the mood right now."

"Not in the mood? You think I give a flying fuck about you being in the mood?" I asked just as a mosquito landed on my cheek and bit me. Immediately, I smacked myself in the face so hard I got mad at myself for doing it, then I transferred that anger back to Roman. "You're the reason my little girl is missing right now. It's all because of you, all because of your negligence!" I yelled so loud in his face preparing for a fight.

He closed his eyes and took a deep breath. I could tell he was trying to maintain his composure and having a hard time doing so. I didn't know what pushing him so far would get me, but I didn't care, either. At that moment all I felt was anger, and I needed to feel some portion of pain.

I was tired of crying and breaking down. I think a part of me just needed a nice ass-whoopin'. The kind of ass-whoopin' I used to get back in the day when Jaheim got mad at me. To me, I didn't think there was anything on earth that would get me on top of my game like an ass-whoopin' from a man. Afterward I was always ready to plot and scheme to my highest potential.

Once again he tried to walk around me, yet I blocked his path. The room was already small. The queen size bed took up most of the space, and there was barely any room left to walk around, so he was pretty much caught between a rock and a hard place He was either about to go through me or stand there and let me remain all in his grill. I knew my cousin wasn't a punk, though. He low-key had a temper so bad back when we were kids our friends called him switch because in one moment he'd be laughing with you, and then in the next he'd have lost his cool and be beating up two dudes at a time in the rawest of fashions. I needed that part of him to come out. I needed for him to beat my ass. I needed to feel some sort of physical pain so the emotional could stop searing my soul.

He took a huge deep breath again. "Tiny, I'm gon' ask you
one more time to get up out of my face, because right now you're acting like I'm the enemy, when I'm not. I made a mistake by letting her out of the house, but what you have to realize is even had I told her not to, she would have gone anyway. All I was trying to do was save face." He shook his head to get a grasp on things. "Had I known that anything like this was about to happen, I would have followed them. This is the worst case scenario." I saw a tear drop from his eye.

"You know what, Roman? I could really hurt you right now. I could really see myself smashing your face in with something heavy because you deserve it. I trusted you, man. I trusted you with my only daughter, and you failed her. I mean, you failed her big time!" I pushed him so hard he flew backward into the door, knocking it partway off of the hinges.

"Holy crap, Mom, what's gotten into you?" Leah said, jumping up from the bed and standing between us. She had a scared look on her face that said she was terrified.

Roman struggled to get up. He grabbed the side of the door to pull himself upward, but that only caused the door to come completely off of its hinges. He slipped once trying to get to his feet, and that must have angered him because the next thing I knew he shot across the room toward me, picked Leah up, and threw her on the bed, where she bounced on it once and then fell off of the other side.

He rushed and picked me up so high in the air my stomach turned upside down, it felt like. My back crashed into the wall, and he held me up there with his hand around my neck, slightly squeezing.

"Listen to me, Tiny. Now, I understand you mad and all that shit, but you ain't about to play me like some fuck-nigga. Now, that's your daughter that's out there missing. I get all of that shit, but the big-ass picture you're missing is the fact she's my little cousin and that I'm crazy about her. I only got to hold her in my arms a few times, and before I could get used to that feeling, she was gone, and I was the one who had given her permission to do such." Tears came down his cheeks. "Now you in here playing me like a sucka, putting your hands on me and shit, and that ain't about to fly. Not now, not ever. If you do it again, I'm gon' take this leather belt off and whoop your ass. I don't care if you are my older cousin, I'm gon' whoop your ass until you come correct, that's my word." He took a deep breath and curled his face. "Now, I'm about to let you down, and if you do anything other than the right thing, your ass is mine. You got that?"

I didn't say a work because obviously I couldn't. I could barely breathe. The only thing on my mind was him putting me down. I already knew that once he did, we was about to tear that room up, because I wanted him to give me a whoopin'. I needed to feel him chastise me. I was just hoping it didn't turn me on the way I was sure it was going too.

I nodded my head and he dropped me to the floor. I landed on my feet, and he turned around to walk away in silence. As soon as his back was turned, I jumped on it and wrapped my arm around his thick neck and bit him on the top of his bald-ass head. The taste of his cologne went all in my mouth and numbed my tongue.

In one quick motion, he flipped me off of his back and onto the bed. He pulled his belt from the loops of his pants and put the buckle in his hand. "Alright, I see what you looking for. Just know I still love your ass."

He held me down and tore my ass up. Afterward, he held me until I fell asleep in his arms with him rubbing my backside and Leah rubbing my feet.

Chapter 4

Roman

I felt extra shitty for what went down with my little cousin. I mean, I felt like the whole ordeal was my fault. I hadn't even had her long enough to get to know her before she was stripped away. Why did life have to be so hard? Why couldn't I ever catch a break? It seemed like every time I tried to leave the life alone, there was always some invisible rope around my ankle pulling me back into it.

I ain't like whooping my cousin's ass, but I low-key knew what she needed to get herself right. I was the one man she wrote to three times a week faithfully. I knew what she liked and what she disliked, and what she needed to get her in the best mind state. I mean, it felt weird doing what I did, but afterward she thanked me, and I couldn't stop her from hugging me and kissing my cheeks. As I was leaving the house, I saw that hint of determination in her eyes, and that got me motivated.

I whipped my Lexus IS F Sport into the right lane and took the dash up to about 70 miles. I had to get this money. I would not be able to focus until I started seeing that cash pile up.

I knocked on the door to my trap house. When it opened, I walked past the young stud with the mask on his face. On his waist were two twin chrome nine-millimeters. He had a blunt in his mouth so big it looked like a dark brown Twinkie on fire. He looked me up and down and smiled.

"Li'l homey, what I tell you about coming to this door with that shit in your mouth?" I asked him, irritated because, in my mind, he was slipping. There was no way possible he would have been able to react in time if he was bum-rushed or blindsided. Even though he had two pistols on his waist, that didn't mean anything in the spur of the moment, because he would still have to grab them out of his waist, cock them, and then shoot. Due to the fact he had a blunt in his mouth, that could cause him to stumble. And if he stumbled, then he was screwed — not only him, but myself, because he was the first line of defense for the trap house.

"Yo, big homey, I'm good. I got this shit under control. You already know how I get down," he said, pulling both pistols from his waistband.

I waited until he did exactly that, then swung and smacked him so hard he did a 180 in the living room, landing on his side.

"Get your ass up and face me."

He slowly came to his knees, then stood up. I grabbed him by the shirt and smashed my forehead against his. "Yo, I give you specific orders because I see shit that you don't. Now, your one very specific command was to not answer my trap with that shit in your mouth, yet you continue to do it, putting me and my establishment in danger." I backhanded him, knelt down, and pulled him up from the floor where he fell. "Don't do it again or your ass is the hood's."

I stood up and looked around the small duplex. Ten other hustlers stood looking over at me with pistols in their hands and eyes wide. There was a big plasma-screened television against the wall with a video game paused on it. That was another thing that pissed me off. I didn't like my hustlers sitting in the house playing video games. How was they supposed to be on point if they got their head in some damn game? I felt the brothers didn't understand every second they sat in that dope spot, their lives were at risk from either death or prison.

Cavali, a heavyset male with dark skin, stepped forward with his arms out. "Say, Roman, I already know you about to snap over this video game being played, but I need you to know we are on point. I haven't been playing the game. I been making sure everything is running smoothly," he said with sweat running down his forehead.

I smiled. "Oh, so you gave the go-ahead for this system to be played while I wasn't around, huh?" I stepped up to him.

I looked around at the other men. When I stepped forward, they stepped back and continued to watch what was going on. It looked so crazy because all of them had their weapons in their hands, and I didn't, yet they seemed to be more afraid than I was.

Cavali went into his pocket and pulled out an asthma pump. He shook it and inhaled the fluids while tilting his head backward. He did it again and put it away. There was so much sweat pouring off of his forehead by now it looked like his scalp was peeing after drinking a whole six-pack of beer.

"Boss, I really didn't give the go-ahead, but I guess I didn't stop them, either," he said, finally wiping some of the water away.

I took a step to the side of him and addressed the rest of the men in the room. "That video game could be the reason one of y'all wind up dying in this joint. When the pressure's on, the man that gets the first jump is usually the one that wins the war or completes the mission. Video games are used in life as distractions from the world. It is impossible to conquer the world, or to complete any task that is set before you, if you are distracted. I give you men strict orders because I understand the game." I looked around at all of them. "This is my trap. I got each and every last one of you muthafuckas eating. All of y'all were project kids without a pot to piss in. Now every last one of you are riding foreign whips with your own cribs and bundles of cash, yet you niggas can't even hold me down enough to listen." I bucked my eyes for dramatic effect.

Cavali spoke up. "You're right, boss, and I apologize on behalf of the whole crew. I promise you all of your rules will be enforced from here on out. I'm the general that you put in charge, so I'll accept my violation on behalf of all of us." He stood before me with his arms wide open.

I admired the moxie in the li'l homey. Balls went a long way with me. Now, I could have violated him by beating him down in front of the other men just to show them I meant business, but to me, all that would have done was created division. Leaders are never supposed to discipline the one you put in charge publically. That shows you have poor decision-making skills. It would also cause him to feel some type of way, and the next thing I know, he'd be hunting me and running my establishment, slowly turning the men against me until it was time for them to finish me.

"Check this out: from here on out just follow my simple commands and we gon' all keep eating real good. Now, we got a major move coming up real soon, and I need to know I can depend on my family." I looked them all over, one face after the next. "Well, can I?"

***

I had $175,000 to my name, but that wasn't counting what I'd gross off of my product. I needed to get right so we could get my little cousin back. The only thing I wished was that I knew where they had her housed, because I'd go in there about thirty deep with assault rifles on my Fourth of July shit. I wanted to murder something about this whole ordeal. In the end, I wanted that fool Jaheim's head on a platter with plenty of crackers and cheese around his shit. That nigga didn't know whose people he was playing with.

I counted the money again and came up with the same total, and it frustrated me. How was I going to come up with $325,000 before the deadline? That had my mind running like crazy. I had to make this happen; there was no doubt in my mind I would. I just didn't know how as of yet. I was thinking about pushing my trap houses to the limit, and even pulling a few kick doors to get my weight up, but that would only cause a whole lot of drama for the long term, which meant once this dilemma with my li'l cousin ended, I'd be forced to clean up all of the other damages I had accrued along the way, not to mention I'd be putting a whole lot of lives in danger, including my own. Chicago was getting grimier and grimier every single day. Niggas was out there playing for keeps, killing their own family in the name of money. Everybody I knew was damn near cutthroat, or had their throats cut by those closest to them. Me personally, I never took life for granted. I knew that in an instant my time could run out, so I tried to make the most of every single day I was blessed to have on this earth.

Emily walked into the room and handed me a glass of lemonade. She was a white girl with features so exotic I just had to give her some wordplay. I met her at the courthouse after coming from one of my many court dates. She had the nerve to be walking up to an Aston Martin. Just as she was about to step in, I grabbed her wrist and thought she would jump out of her skin. Instead, all she did was give me a smile. That blew my wig back, because the city of Chicago had a high crime surge of car jackings, so I expected this broad to have screamed or tried to run or something, but she did none of the above.

After we got to know each other, I found out she was a pure adrenalin junky. She loved to live life on the edge, and the crazier the situation, the better. Her father was the Assistance District Attorney in Chicago, and he was on the verge of becoming the head and first in charge. Her mother, on the other hand, was an old actress back in Paris. She had even played on a few sitcoms here in America. Long story short, this broad was loaded up with cash, but she was also loaded down with a drug problem. Every time we were together, she was either snorting something up her nose or shooting something into her veins. That was one of the reasons I couldn't see myself putting my dick in her. Our relationship was built around her fascination of the size of my penis. She had an obsession with it. She loved to hold it, suck on it, and talk too it like it would be able to give her some sort of sound advice. At first it was a little weird, but then she bought me a Range Rover fresh out of the lot and put ten gees in my pocket and called it walking-around money. After that, whenever she wanted to hold my dick, I made sure I was available.

She handed me the lemonade, knelt down and put her head in my lap, pulling out my penis and sucking its long length. After making a nasty sucking noise, she said, "There is just something about black dick this big that drives me absolutely insane." She licked it and ran it all over her lips. Revealing her teeth, she slightly bit the head. "I love all of these thick vein, and how I can barely hold it with one hand. It's so fat and heavy. It's like your mother got impregnated by a horse. I need to feel it inside of me, so why won't you fuck my white pussy?" She popped me back into her mouth and swallowed until she gagged.

I had to play this bitch without losing her. There wasn't one ounce of me that wanted to fuck her. I really didn't like white girls like that. I don't know why, I just never did. I think maybe it had something to do with the fact my old man left my mother for one back in the day, and she never got over it. Every day she always spoke about how much he'd hurt her. That and the fact I just loved sistahs and exotic women. I didn't think there was a finer woman on this earth than the black woman, and I mean the black woman in all her shades and hues. I loved them to death. Second was Spanish women. I had a low-key thing for them, too.

She squeezed my thigh and continued to beg me.

"Emily, you know I respect you way too much to put my dick inside of you without marrying you first. You are a damn good woman, and you are to be treasured. I put my dick inside of whores, not a goddess."

I hated talking to this broad like that. I hated uplifting this bitch in any fashion at all because she did not deserve to be uplifted. I always tried to reserve my jewels for my sistahs who were held down by the world her race of men

41

ran. I knew I would never marry her – that shit never crossed my mind, not even for the money. I simply needed to keep the mental manipulations going while I got what I was getting. I needed to ask this broad to hit me like never before, and the last thing I needed was for her to have a bipolar episode.

"But I don't want to be a goddess. I want you to fuck me so hard I bleed. I want this big dick all the way up inside my white pussy, and I want it right now, so stop playing with me." She stood and pulled her dress upward, exposing her hairless pink sex lips. Reaching under herself, she spread herself wide, preparing to sit on my pipe.

I caught her by the hips and stood up. "Whoa, hold on there, shorty. I told you I had to holler at you about some important business. I can't focus on shit until we get this business sorted out. Now, you gotta respect that," I said, watching her slide two fingers into her center.

"Okay, but then you have to fuck me with all of your might. I feel like it's just time. I need you to put that black meat inside of me and fuck me like the slave master's daughter, please!"

I couldn't help but smile. I couldn't wrap my head around fucking her, but if I had to, then I most definitely would. I would do anything to get that paper my li'l cousin needed. I knew this broad had access to those kinds of funds, so in that moment she was my only hope.

Chapter 5

Roman

"I need $500,000 by the end of this week, and there is no way around it. My cousin has been kidnapped, and her ransom is 500 gees. I need to know if you're going to help me or if I'm going to have to figure something out, but either way, I gotta make it happen for her, because she needs me." I looked her over closely to gauge her body language. Her eyes were open so big I could see the pinks of her eyelids.

"500 grand? Holy fuck, Roman! Have you lost your mind?" Now her fingers were out of her pussy and she started to pace the floor. She sighed. "And what makes you think I have access to that kind of money?" She said this without looking me in the face.

On some real shit, I wanted to go in on her and just verbally break her ass down because here we were in a big-ass mansion, sitting on the side of a pool with glasses of lemonade on a crystal table top. To get back here on the terrace, I walked past a tennis court and a mini-golf field. To my left was a full basketball court, and directly up the pathway from that was where she kept her horses. The entire interior of the house was decked out in Burberry, and that included the seats to her Aston Martin. Her fingernails were even painted and designed by Burberry. So, I didn't feel like playing these kinds of games with her. I just didn't have the patience.

"Emily, you know I have a lot of respect for you, and ever since you and I have been talking, I have always tried to keep shit real with you. I sincerely need your help.

Now, I don't know whether you have the money or not, but what I do know is I need you."

She ran her fingers through her blonde hair and shook her head. Reaching into her bra, she pulled out a package of white powder. She sat at the table and poured the contents over the crystal top, dipped her pinky finger into it, and scooped a heavy portion up with her fingernail and tooted it up her nose. She snorted hard and did the same thing with the other nostril. She pulled her nose, then ran some of the powder across her teeth. Rolling her head around on her shoulders, she closed her eyes and bit into her bottom lip. "Roman, I really want to help you, but that is a lot of money. I wouldn't even know how to address my parents for that amount. That's serious." She sighed out loud for dramatic effect.

I sat there beside her big-ass pool with the sun shining down on me, listening to her horses neighing off in the distance. Seven seagulls flew up in the sky overhead, and the sound of their gardener could be heard mowing their lawn in the front.

Something in me just snapped.

I shot up from my seat and grabbed this white bitch by her hair and pushed her face into the table roughly. "I know what you want me to do, bitch. I know you want me to treat yo' pink ass, so that's what's gon' happen." I got behind her and kicked her legs apart. With her chest laying on the table top, that left her ass all the way up in the air. I yanked her Burberry cheerleading skit all the way up her hips and yanked her panties off of her, baring her tanned ass cheeks. In one motion I put my hand all the way up in the air and brought it down at full speed, smacking her so hard on the ass she yelped out in pain and spread her legs further.

"Oh, fuck! Roman, please do that shit again. Please, fucking smack my ass as hard as you can and treat me like your white whore. Please, treat me like the slut I am," she screamed.

I slapped her ass again and again, trying to smack the skin off of her shit. The harder I slapped it, I noticed the wetter she became. It got to the point where I saw her juices running down her legs as if she were peeing on herself. Seeing that and hearing how she was talking was starting to turn me on.

She got to rubbing her clitoris real hard and bouncing her ass against my hand. "Fuck me now, Roman! Please, I'll do anything. I'll get your fucking money, just fuck me right now as hard as you can. I need you to violate me and punish me for being a white, privileged whore!" She spread her legs wide and ripped her bathing suit top off, exposing a fake pair of perky breasts with hard nipples.

I was already ahead of schedule. I ripped the condom packet with my teeth, spit out the wrapper, slid it onto my penis, and rammed it into her so hard she screamed out at the top of her lungs. I dug my nails into her hips and proceeded to fuck her with all of my might while I pulled on her blonde extensions. There was so much discarded hair in a pile by my feet it was liked I had just finished sweeping the floor at a beauty salon. I mean, I was pulling all of her shit out.

She bounced back into me and continued to make noises as if she were possessed. She held her backside open and kept smacking herself on the cheeks. "Put it in there, Roman. Stretch me right there. If you put it up there, I'll figure out your situation, one way or the other. I just want your black dick up there so bad. I want my slave to fuck me and make me his slave, so do it, baby! Fuck me up there like you hate me!" she screamed.

I got to imagining the movie *Roots* while I fucked the white, privileged shit out of her. I mean, I fucked her so bad that when it was all over and done with, she ran and soaked her ass in the pool. I had to laugh at that while I showered in her father's personal bathroom.

Before I left, she promised me she'd be in touch when she had her hands on the money, I felt like I had accomplished a major mission.

***

Tiny

My mind was racing a million miles a second, and I didn't know how to slow it down. I could not stop panicking as each hour passed away and I still didn't have a solution to the problem. I did all I could to clear my mind so I actually could focus on something else for a few minutes, but nothing worked.

I sat on Roman's porch next to Jackie and watched her as she swatted away a bee that had flown directly into her face. She jumped up and ran, and that caused me to do the same thing. The last thing I needed was to be stung by a nasty-ass bee when I was allergic to their kind. It was so hot outside it felt like my head was in an oven roasting. I didn't have any panties on, and my kitten was still hot.

I watched the bee chase Jackie in her little shorts, the bottom halves of her ass cheeks shaking every time she moved the slightest. The bee must have finally left her alone, because she made her way back up the steps with sweat pouring down her forehead.

Ariana came out of the house with a big, iced pitcher of blue Kool-Aid. She handed out glasses with crushed ice in them and poured the Kool-Aid on top of it. I took one sip and felt like my mouth had been saved from a desert storm. The cool liquid, for a second, took my cares away. It was so humid it felt like I had a sweater on.

"Do you feel better, momma?" Ariana asked, kissing me on the forehead. She sat down beside me with shorts on so small they basically disappeared, and both of her thighs were completely bared.

"Yeah, thanks, baby. I feel a lot better than I did. You're amazing." I leaned my forehead against hers and left it covered with sweat. Before I drank the Kool-Aid, it looked like somebody hit me in the face with a water balloon.

I stood up and fanned my face with my hand, looking out into the neighborhood. It seemed like everybody was out on their porch trying to get some air. Little boys were chasing each other with water guns and water balloons, and there was an occasional girl targeted as well. There were a couple adult males working on the fire hydrant to get it to squirt all the way up in the air. Once they succeeded with that mission, all of the women on the block seemed to come out of their houses in bikinis to get some of the cool water play. Even I thought about it for a second before Alexis overtook my thoughts. There were little girls on the sidewalk jumping double-dutch and singing their nursery rhymes along with the rope play. A few boys were yelling and screaming as they threw the football around with no shirts on.

"Dang, that water look fun," Jackie said, standing up and dusting her butt off. I couldn't help but stare because her shorts had been swallowed by all that brown ass. I could only imagine what a man would think if all that got wet up with the water. She looked up at me as if she wanted me to give her permission to go play, and I simply nodded.

Ariana's phone rang and she answered it almost immediately, stepping down from the porch. She walked back and forth, talking with her hands. When she hung up, she ran over to me and seemed to be excited. "Momma, I just called in a major connect, and I'm going to see if he'll help us with our situation with Alexis. I know he has a lot of money, and he really likes me." She wrapped her arms around herself. "I have to go into the house and get dressed. I cannot let him see me looking all popped like this."

She was on her way back into the house when I stopped her and blocked her path. "Are you out of your mind, little girl? Do you honestly think I am going to let you out of my sight without you telling me who this man is?" I asked just as a fly flew into my ear and got stuck there. The buzzing irritated me so bad I screamed, and that still did not make the fly get out of it. It tried to go up my ear canal until I twisted my head and sort of dug it out. Only then did it fly away, but by that time I was freaked out.

I opened the door to the house and went in, feeling the air conditioning slap me in the face. I started to feel like a fool for sitting out on the hot porch when I had a whole cool house to chill in.

"Mom, you need not worry. This guy is pretty famous. I'm sure as soon as you see who he is, you'll give him your full approval. I just want you to keep in mind I am working a specific angle here. I know I need to do my part to help my sister out. We have to free her from the grips of that monster." She shook her head slowly, and turned on her toes, on her way up the stairs.

I grabbed ahold of her arm. "Wait a minute, little girl. Just because you've said what you have, that doesn't mean I have made my decision one way or the other." I scratched my shoulder and looked to where it was itching me. I wondered if I had been bitten by a mosquito while I was outside. They were everywhere now.

Ariana grunted, "Okay, so what are you saying? Are you saying you want to meet with him first, and then you'll give me your permission?" she asked with her eyes seemingly pleading for mercy.

By this time I had scratched the spot on my arm so much it looked like it was ready to bleed. I looked down at it and said, "You have to understand, I have already had one daughter taken from me. I would seriously lose my mind if something happened to you. I love you so fucking much." I had tears rolling down my cheeks before I even knew it.

She ran to me and hugged me so tight I let out a little gas. "Mom, I love you, too, and I promise you'll approve of this guy. He's a professional basketball player. He plays for the Bulls. He has a whole lot of money, and I know he won't be afraid to give me some, I'm going to try and get as much as possible for my sister." She took a step back and kissed me on the cheek.

"I understand what you're saying, Ariana, but if you think you're going anywhere tonight, you better be prepared for me to be right beside you."

Three hours later, we were in a fucking helicopter circling the skyline of Chicago. I could not believe my eyes when Ariana's male friend pulled up in a Range Rover limousine with a chauffeur. He respectively came onto the porch and knocked on the door, asking for her. I answered it and could not believe how tall and well-dressed he was. His cologne was on point, and he was quite handsome. I also was taken aback by his manners, which were also on point. Once Ariana came down the stairs, we all got acquainted, and the end result was me riding out with them.

The skyline always reminded me of how beautiful Chicago looked on the surface. It was an illusion. It would make the average person think this city was full of hope and promise, when in reality this was a city that daily sucked the life out of the living. This city broke heart, and caused constant pains. I had watched so many of my closest friends, and their friends and family die here, and not of old age. This city was deadly, and it taught people how to be their own portion of deadly to survive in it.

I didn't know what Ariana's whole game plan was, but I truly believed she would be okay for the night without me. This guy seemed as if he had a lot of class. I asked them if they'd drop me back off at the house. I was feeling so out of place. I just wanted to get home so I could collect my thoughts.

"What's the matter, Momma? Aren't you having a good time? Or do you want to go somewhere else? I'm sure it isn't a problem, right, Noah?" she said, looking the man over closely.

He smiled calmly. " I am enjoying your company, Ms. Johnson. You being here does not taint the mood at all." He reached and grabbed my hand. "Just let me know if there is anything further I can do for you, and I will not hesitate to make it happen."

He kissed the back of my hand, and that made me feel some type of way. I had to get away from him or I was going to be eating my daughter's man up.

"Well, I am completely flattered. It's just I have a lot on my mind, and I need to cook dinner for the rest of the family. I have really enjoyed myself for one evening. Now, I think its time you two kids were left alone."

When I got back home, there was a BMW 530i in front of the house. Jackie stood leaning into the window with her daisy dukes all in her butt. As soon as I got out of the limousine, the interior lights came on inside the car and a male stepped out with a neck full of jewelry. I sized him up quickly and tried to make my way into the house, calling Jackie to do the same.

"Say, aren't you Tiny? Aren't you Alexis' mother?" he asked, trying to close the gap between us with speed.

My heart began to beat faster. I didn't know who he was or why he was asking me these questions. I motioned for Jackie to come into the house, then turned around to face him just as I opened the door to our house. "And who might you be?" I asked.

"My name is Li'l Chris, and your daughter and my best friend have been abducted by the same people. I need to know who they are and how we can wipe them off of the face of this earth after we get our people back."

T.J. & Jelissa

Chapter 6

Ariana

"Yes, grip my neck tighter. Stop playing with me. I want you to really choke me like you got that shit in you," I commanded of Noah. He had me up against the wall in our royal suite at the Waldorf Astoria with his hands around my neck. I told him I wasn't giving him no pussy, and he decided to get an attitude. So, I told him to take me home, and this fool had the nerve to slap me and throw me against the wall, so now I guess what came next was him choking me. "I ain't scared of you, rich boy. You're pussy. You don't even know how to choke somebody."

I reached and slapped him. That made him drop his hands from around my neck. I took that as my cue to run, so I did. I got as far as the door before he grabbed my leg and pulled me across the floor like I was an unruly child.

"You yellow bitch. You think I'm about to fly you all around Chicago with your mother and not get nothing for it? You must be out of your fucking mind." He dove on top of me and ripped my Valentino dress down the middle. He put his hand around my neck and squeezed. Leaning forward, he licked the side of my face. "I'm gon' fuck this hot pussy nice and hard. I mean, I'm gon' make you come so much you're gon' faint every time you see my team play on television."

I felt him going between my legs and trying to pull my panties down. I pressed my thighs together to try to make it hard for him while I felt him maneuvering himself to open the fly to his expensive Italian pants.

"Let me go, Noah! Don't do me like this. I'm not that kind of girl." I tried to shake him off of me, but he was too strong.

After getting tired of wrestling with me to get my panties down, he simply pulled them to the side and slid his finger deep within my channel, first one, and then the second. He moaned into my ear after he felt how hot my cave was.

"Please, don't do this," I whined.

He forced my legs open further, positioned himself, and ran his huge penis up and down in between my sex lips. "Oh, just look at how wet you are, Ariana. I can tell you like that I'm taking this pussy from you. Tell me you love how I'm forcing you to give it to me."

I felt him plunge deep into me, and I couldn't help but scream and hump my ass off the floor.

"Tell me, bitch!"

"Okay, yes, I love how you're taking my pussy. I love how you're fucking me so hard it hurts me. Fuck me harder! Please, fuck me as hard as you can. I need you to hurt my pussy, daddy!" I cried with real tears coming down my cheeks. By this time he was fucking me at full speed, putting a hurting on my little cave. He licked my earlobe and bit into my neck, forcing my juices to shoot out of me in globs.

"Yeah, bitch, daddy knows. Daddy knows you love his dick, don't you? You love when I take this pussy from you every time I am around you. This shit belongs to me, don't it?"

He flipped me onto my stomach, pushed my right knee upward, and dove into me from behind so hard all I could hear in the room was the sound of our skins slapping together. It sounded like somebody was getting hit repeatedly on the back by an open hand. It got even better when he started to spank me and pull my hair. It ended with me up against the wall and him biting my neck so hard the he left teeth marks there for three whole days.

Afterward, we lay cuddled up by the fireplace on a bearskin rug, sipping strawberry champagne. I was trying to muster up the courage to ask him what I needed to. I knew money really wasn't an object for him, but I still did not want to sound like the average gold digger. I knew my sister needed that cash, though, and I was willing to do anything to get it for her. I just had to pick the right time.

He leaned over me and sucked on my bottom lip. His huge log rubbed against my naked stomach and made me get butterflies. His body was incredible. I mean, I loved the way it felt, and looked, and even tasted. He had me hooked on basketball players, for real.

"What's the matter, baby? You haven't said a word in, like, 30 full minutes." He rubbed my chin and kissed me on the cheek.

I heard what he'd said, but my mind had taken me back to when I'd first met him. Our foster grandparents had decided to quit being cheap and take us all to a basketball game in the city. I really did not like basketball, and I tried everything within my willpower to not go; however, the end result did not fair well for me. At least, that is what I thought in the beginning.

Anyway, long story short, I wound up going. After the game, my foster brother decided to run on to the court. He was only seven years old. I chased him, and he ran directly into the arms of Noah as he was on his way into the locker room. That is where we met, and we had been seeing each other off and on ever since then whenever he could get away from his job and his pregnant wife he already had two kids with.

He kissed me again and ran his fingers through my long, curly hair, pulling it away from my face. He kissed me right on the cheek and positioned his penis so it slowly worked itself back into me.

I moaned and felt him hit that deepness so many could not. He grabbed the meat of my ass and fucked me hard while pulling my hair. I couldn't help screaming like he was killing me. I felt him deep within my stomach, and I loved the feeling. I started throwing my butt back into his lap while he gripped my hips with his big hands.

"Fuck, Ariana, this pussy is so good. Every single stroke of this shit drives me crazy. I gotta duck you off somewhere. I gotta make you my number-one mistress. I'm gon' cash you for having a box this great!"

He pulled me up to my knees and slammed me into him while I huffed and puffed and spread my ass for him. I felt him coming deep within my channel, and that pushed me over the top. I came screaming and pulling patches out of the rug.

We had just stepped out of the shower when he snatched me up and sucked on my earlobe. He handed me a jewelry box.

"Baby, these are for you." He wrapped his hands around my waist while I stood in front of him.

I couldn't believe my eyes when I opened the box and saw the pink lemonade earrings that had to be nearly a full carat. They glistened in the light, looking like pink, shiny disco balls. The more I turned them around in my hands, the more I became enamored with them. I felt guilty about asking what I needed to now, but I had to.

"Baby, these are beautiful. I mean, I really love them."

"I knew you would. And you deserve them. You're my Midwest Honey, so I gotta always take care of you."

He hugged me from the back and I sighed in defeat. He turned me around to look into my face. Taking his thumb, he ran it across my cheek. "Baby, what's the matter?"

I took both of his wrists in my hands while he looked me directly in the eyes. " My sister has been kidnapped, and her ransom is $500,000. Me and my mother have no way of getting her back. I need your help, but I have been afraid to ask you all night long." I looked at the floor, and then up and into his eyes.

He released me and even pushed me a little bit. "Really, Ariana?" He gave me a menacing look. "Bitch, that's the best line you can come up with, that you sister has been taken away and she needs $500,000 for a ransom? Really, man?" He scoffed and looked at me from the side of his face.

I started to panic. "But, Noah, I swear to you I'm not lying. If you want, I can have my mother get on the phone and tell you the same thing." I ran over to the bed and knelt down to grab my phone out of my purse.

"Oh, so you think because your mother run the same script, you hos about to get a half of a million dollars out of me? You better call her over here and both of you bitches better put on the show of your lives," he snickered. "Get dressed. I'm dropping your ratchet-ass off back into the slums where you belong." He walked past me and bumped me so hard I turned a little.

I grabbed his arm and turned him around. "Look, you stupid son of a bitch, I'm not lying to you. And you can say whatever you want about me, but you better put some respect on my mother. Now, all you had to do was say no. All this extra shit is way too much. Check yo'self, for real." I turned around to start getting dressed.

"Bitch, who the fuck you think you're talking to like that? In case you don't remember, you're in my high-priced-ass hotel. I'm the one footing the bill for you. Burning fuel flying your ratchet-ass all around Chicago just so I could make a good impression on your mother, and all along both of you bitches got an agenda."

I walked up on him and pushed him so hard he fell over the bed. "Fuck-nigga, say something else about my mother and I swear I'm gon' kill your ass. Now, try me."

I continued putting my clothes on. I was just sliding my ripped dress back into place when he smacked me so hard I went out cold.

When I awoke, he was standing over me with his dick out, pissing on my forehead. I tried my best to get from under him, but I was too woozy.

After he finished, he shook his dick and pulled his pants up.

"You sick son of a bitch. I got you."

He picked me up and threw me into the pool, then took the beach ball and hit me in the face with it. "That's what I think about your half-gold-digging-ass. Bitch, you need to get your mind right. I can't believe you even had the nerve to try me like that. Bitch gon' ask me for 500 gees. Bitch, my wife can't even get 10 percent of that, so why in the fuck would I give that to you? Your pussy good, but it ain't life-changing money good."

I climbed out of the pool, and this fool gon' run and drop kick me right back into it. I was so pissed off I wanted to kill him. I had made the worst mistake by letting down my guard with this clown. He was proof that no matter how much money a man had, if their core was rotten, then so would they be.

T.J. & Jelissa

Chapter 7

Roman

"But I understood everything you were putting down. It's just that sometimes I get hardheaded," Cavali said, sitting in the passenger seat of my truck. He bit into his cheeseburger and stuffed some fries into his mouth so he could eat them all together.

I turned my head sideways so I could take a nice, big bite of my gyro. We were at Jennifer's Red Hots, and I was so hungry I could have eaten off the floor and felt okay about it. I was starving, and I needed my stomach fed. I sucked from the straw and allowed the lemon lime pop to quench my thirst. I took my fork and shoved some chili cheese fries into my mouth as well.

"You know, Cavali, I give you a great deal of trust and respect. Ain't I one of the reasons you're no longer struggling in them projects?" I asked with a mouth full of food.

"Ain't no doubt about it. I would be out here starving if it wasn't for you." He took another huge bite if his burger and stuffed his mouth with fries. "You know, Roman, when that fool King and Chris forced my parents to inject that shit into their arms, I didn't know what I was going to do, man. My mother was strung out, my pops was stealing everything out of the crib, and my mother was selling her body to every nigga in the hood. And there I was, nine years old, without a pot to piss in. And then you came along."

"It's not that I came along, it's that I was a part of it all because them niggas hit my parents up, too." I shook my head and tried to shake out the cobwebs.

"I know you gotta have a reason for bringing me out tonight, so I guess I'm just trying to figure out what it is. That been on my mind this whole time, I can barely enjoy this burger. I mean, it's good and all, but my tongue can't really enjoy it until I know why I'm out here," he said, taking another bite and reaching for his drink. He grabbed the pop and shook it from side to side. I could here the ice inside of it sloshing around.

I wiped my fingers on a few napkins and sat back in my seat, looking over at him. He was a man of about 250 pounds, more muscle than fat. He stood about 5 feet, 10 inches tall with skin so black that when he closed his eyes, his whole face looked like the period at the end of a sentence. His temper was as bad as mine, if not hotter, yet he was also a thinker.

I remembered when I met him in the projects way back when. I found him and his sister eating out of the garbage can. What made me take a shine to him was even though he was two years younger than his sister, he was the one inside the metal can, handing the food out to her, making sure she got something in her stomach first. I found them behind our project building at 4:00 in the morning. A crazy drunk bum stood a few feet off in the distance, watching them closely. The same bum would be labeled the project rapist three months later. There was no doubt in my mind that had I not taken them with me that day, the Bum would have done something real sick to them kids. I was only six years older than him, but I was already in the game, hustling under a fool named Draylon who had me eating real good. King and Chris wound up killing him and taking over the buildings where we lived.

Things were real crazy back then. Nearly everyone's parents in our project building were literally held down and injected with a strong heroin-based drug. After all of that happened, our city went downhill fast. Cavali had been working under me every since then, even when I had to pull a few bits in the pen. I trusted him, and I respected his gangsta, but that had never stopped me from getting on his ass when I needed too.

We sat in the parking lot, watching the patrons go in and out of the restaurant. It was so hot people were sweating out there like crazy. Most of them looked like they came straight from basketball practice. There were big sweat stains on the back of their shirts and every thing. I turned the AC up in the truck a little higher.

"I need to know if I can trust you, Cavali?" I said, grabbing my pop and sucking it through the straw.

He was putting the garbage into his food bag after wiping his hands on a napkin. He put a fist up to his mouth and burped so loud I thought the airbag was going to deploy. Hitting a fist on his chest, he laughed and shook his head. "My bad, Roman, but you know what that good eating do." He dropped the trash out of the window, then rolled it back up and sat snuggly in his seat. Looking over at me with eyes wide, he said, "The fact you feel you have to ask me this question hurts my heart. I mean, you have been there for me like no other, with the exception of my sister." He shook his long dreads, and flipped them over his shoulder. "Yo, I'd give my life for you in a heartbeat, with no question about it. That's my word." He pulled out a cigar filled with weed so big it looked like a mini sub sandwich.

I shook my head and looked him over closely. "I do trust you, and I got a lot of love for you, man." I nodded my head and took another sip of my pop. I looked out my window and saw a heavyset girl pushing a stroller with a baby inside of it. She was just about to go inside of Jennifer's Red Hots when a dude pulled up alongside her with his car and jumped out and got into her face. He kept reaching down inside of the stroller, and she was pulling his hands from inside of it. I couldn't hear what they were saying, but clearly the dispute was over the child.

"I'm ready to move on them fools down the block, and I want you to run point with me." I kept my eyes on the confrontation outside of my window. Now the man was face-to-face with the chubby chick, but she wasn't backing down. She had her finger all in his face, talking a mile a minute. "My li'l cousin been snatched up, and a muthafucka talking about they want 500 stacks in order to release her. Now, I got some things in the works on another end, but I just can't put all of my eggs into one basket. Them niggas down the block been in the way for way too long anyway. I hear they stepping on they product excessively, and that's causing the whole block to look back because the fiends aren't able to know for sure if they're going to get their bunk dope or our flame. It's just too big of a risk for them, and times are hard, so when a dopehead decide to spend their money, they want to make sure they are getting quality and quantity. Not only that, but I got word them niggas are already planning on moving on us when they get their weight up a little more. It's best we eradicate that situation before it becomes more of a problem." I curled my lip. "Can you understand what I am saying to you?"

He fidgeted in his seat and blew air out of his nose before briefly putting his thumb and forefinger over it. " Yo, quiet as kept, I been wanting to get up with them fools' glamour anyway. Shit been hectic every since that nigga Moan kicked Lacey to the curb after he put his hands all on her. I took that as a sign of disrespect right then." He frowned, took his Tech .9 from under the seat, and placed it on his lap. "Yo, it's like I got this feeling in me that needs to kill something all the time. I be itching, Roman, so all you gotta do is tell me what you need for me to do." He lit the cigar and inhaled deeply.

I let my window down a bit. I was trying to keep my distance from that sticky. I had so many tasks to master that the last thing I needed was any type of high. I needed to be focused at all times.

"I wanna move on them niggas this weekend. You see that nigga Moan fuck with one of my connects, and I know he strap up to go get his product every Sunday. That fool stacks his paper for three weeks straight, and then he ride out to Riverdale with about 150 thousand to get his weight up. I wanna snatch the product and the paper, while at the same time leaving that fool with more lead in him than a number 2 pencil, you feel me?"

Cavali rubbed his chin and nodded his head up and down. "Yo, I'm wit' it, boss. Anything you need for me to do, I'm gon' do it. That's fucked up about your li'l cousin, though. I already know we finna tear some shit up over that."

He bit into his bottom lip, looking out my window. By this time there was a whole group of girls standing behind the chubby one. They had the slim man cornered. The chubby girl reached into her purse and came up with a box cutter so fast it was like I was watching her do magic. She swung the weapon and sliced the dude straight across his face. His blood skeeted out onto the concrete, and she tackled him with the other girls jumping in. Before I knew it, they had him on the ground, stomping a mud hole into his ass.

"Yo, Roman, let's get the fuck up out of here before Chicago's finest roll up."

Just as he said that, we heard a popping noise. I looked over to where they were stomping the man and saw two girls fall flat on their backs. The chubby chick reached into the stroller to grab her baby. I saw the man they were stomping getting up with a gun in his hand. He pointed it directly at her and pulled the trigger, hitting her close range in the shoulder. That twisted her around, but not enough to make her drop her child. She took off running one way, and he ran another. The women hit by his first shots lay on the ground unmoving.

I backed the truck up and sped away getting a more firm understanding with Cavali. I needed to make sure we were on the same page with everything, because things had to take place fast.

***

Tiny

I woke up to the sounds of the front door being beat on so loud I thought it was the police coming to tell me they had found my baby somewhere dead. Every part of me felt like it was ready to lock up, I was terrified.

I threw a robe around myself, and made my way to the door with Leah behind me. It seemed like everywhere I went, she was always just a few paces behind.

Right before I got to the door, the banging started again. Now I was really getting paranoid. "Hold on, here I come!" I yelled, but slowing my paces. I finally got there and took a deep breath opening the door. I didn't even know I was holding my breath until I started to get dizzy.

Ariana shot right into the house in a frenzy. "That son of a bitch has put his hands on me for the last time!" she screamed, walking into the living room. I followed close behind her with Leah on my heels.

Ariana continued to pace back and forth with her hands balled into fists. I could see she had a huge, red handprint on one of her cheeks. I walked up to her and forced her to be still while I checked it out. Up that close, I could also see her lip was split.

"What the hell happened? Did Noah do this?" I asked, trying to wrap my head around that reality. When I left their sides, they both looked so in love and so happy. How did all of this manage to transpire? What did I miss? I had clearly read him all wrong.

"Yeah, that dirtbag did all of this. He did all of this because I told him about Alexis and he didn't believe me. He thought I was trying to trick him into giving us 500 grand just for the sport of it." She put her hand to her cheek and winced in pain. " Geez, why do guys always have to beat a girl? Like, what is it with them?" There were tears running down her cheeks. For the first time I noted her dress was all ripped and torn. That made a bell go off in my head.

"Wait a minute, Ariana. Did you guys have sex last night?" I asked, hoping for the right answer.

She looked a bit uncomfortable. "Mom, I am 18. I mean, if I had, I wouldn't have been doing anything wrong, right?"

"No, baby, you wouldn't have. But if you had, we're definitely going to make him pay," I said, looking her over. Her neck was excessively red, and there were bite marks all over it. There was a handprint on her face, and I could see noticeable bruising along her wrists.

"Wait, I don't get it. How would me being 18 and having sex with him make him pay?" she asked, looking confused. She turned and sat down on the couch with her knees together. It looked like she even had bruises up along her thighs.

I yelled for Leah to go and bring me her phone, and when she did, I started taking one picture after the next.

"Mom, what are you doing? Why are you taking pictures of me?" she hollered, trying to cover herself up.

"Don't you get it, baby? This man just abused and beat you up." I continued to take more pictures. "Tell me, where did you guys go last night?" I peeled back the straps of her dress some so I could take pictures of the bruises on her chest and thighs.

"We went to the Waldorf Astoria and stayed in for the rest of the night." She blushed after revealing this intimate detail.

"If there is one thing I know about that hotel, it's that they are extremely tight on security. They must have a thousand images with you two together. We're going to make this fuck-nigga pay. I know y'all had to have had sex. Have you taken a shower or anything yet since then?"

"No, but he did throw me into the pool. Wait, but then again, that wouldn't matter because he savagely screwed me again after that and pissed in my face." She placed her face within the palms of her hands. "Why do things like this always have to happen to me?" she whined. Leah knelt down beside her and rubbed her back. They stayed that way for a few seconds, then out of the blue she stuck up her head and gave me a crazy look. "Mom, what are you thinking, and why are you asking such weird questions?"

All I could do was smile. "You need to get your mind right, because I'm calling the police. I have a plan that cannot fail."

***

It was three days later, and the chaos had not died down from this situation. Ariana was approached by so many people from the media trying to cover this story that it was all starting to go to her head. They offered her large sums of money, but nowhere near the amount we needed for her to give their network an exclusive. More than twice she almost took the bait, but I stopped her from doing so. We had to move in a very strategic manner, and I had to stay on top of things.

We were coming back from seeing an attorney that had decided to pick up her case when Li'l Chris swerved his car and parked crazily behind us and jumped out with his arms in the air. I thought he had lost his mind or something.

"Yo, what up, Ms. Johnson? I hope you're ready to sit down and have a little lunch, because I wanna take you out." He paused. "I mean, if that's okay with you."

Jackie stepped out of the passenger's seat and stood in front of me, popping back on her slightly bowed legs. Her jeans were so tight I could see the dimples in the side of her booty. "I hope you planning on taking all of us out, because Ms. Johnson ain't the only one that's hungry." She placed her hand on her hip, and sucked on her bottom lip.

He looked her up and down and licked his thick lips. His eyes ran over her body again and again, and then he grabbed his crotch. "Yo, on some real shit, though, you can come anywhere we're about to go. Matter fact, after I finish talking this business with Ms. Johnson, I wanna take you to the mall and cash you out. I'll foot the bill for whatever you're trying to do, that's my word." He reached into his pocket and pulled out a bankroll of hundreds and flashed it at her.

She rolled her eyes. "What's that supposed to mean? Just because you're showing it don't mean you're going to spend it on me." She crossed her arms over her chest and gave him a look that said she was unimpressed.

He squinted his eyes and gave her look that said he was serious. "Here, catch this and go put it in the house. That's yours. All I ask is you spend some quality time with me later." He turned to me. "Ms. Johnson, can me and you go and have a sit-down?"

I was still perplexed by the fact he'd just flexed on Jackie in a cold fashion. He had to have given her about $10,000 like it wasn't nothing. That blew my mind and had my pussy a little wet, to be honest. I started to look at him in a new light. "Yeah, Chris, let's go and have lunch. I mean, as long as you're treating," I smiled.

Jackie held onto the money as if she could not believe it was really real. She stood frozen in place, seeming like she didn't know what to do. Finally, she stuffed the knot in her bra and nodded. "Yeah, Chris, me and you can definitely get together later on. I think we have a lot to discuss." She winked at him, and I thought it was so corny, but he laughed and nodded his agreement.

Chapter 8

Ariana

I was steaming from what Noah had done to me. I couldn't believe he would treat me the way he did. I mean, how many people would come up with a story like that? How many people would ask for that sum of money? It just didn't make sense, and he should have known that. I had never been more frustrated than I was in that moment.

My mother seemed as if she knew what she was doing with everything, so I decided to keep it in her hands. Every night she would lace me with some new game on how to react and respond to the questioning and media attention. Even though I cared about Noah, I cared about my sister way more. My mother said we were going to be able to hit his pockets three times worse than what I originally asked him for. I didn't know how or when, but she seemed like she did, so that was cool by me.

I took a nice, hot shower, got out still moist, and decided to moisturize my body from head to toe. I slid on my nice, tight, pink boy shorts that hugged my muffin in the front and my ass in the back. I slid my pink beater over my head, deciding against wearing a confining bra. I felt the girls needed to breathe. The house was nice and quiet. I didn't know where everybody was, but I really didn't care. I could use a little peace and tranquility.

I had just lay down on my back with some soft R&B playing when I heard the front door slam. A part of me got extremely irritated right away because I felt like there was never any alone time in the house. I heard Roman's voice, and that made me perk up. I shot out of the room, and paused at the top of the stairs to hear him better.

"Hello? I know everybody ain't gone. That shit never happens around here."

I heard some moving about down there where he was and decided to make my way down the flight of stairs, pinching my nipples through my beater. "Roman, who are you down there talking to?" I asked. I stepped onto the carpet and headed in his direction.

He was in the kitchen with the refrigerator open. He reached in and came out with a small container of orange juice. At seeing me, he smiled. "Hey there, li'l momma. What are you doing in the house all by yourself?" He held out his arms so I could walk into them.

I damn near broke my neck trying to get to him. I needed to feel his big muscles wrapped around my small body. I needed to feel protected and loved, and I felt like he was the only male who could show me that.

As soon as he wrapped me within his embrace, I smelled his cologne, and it made my kitty quiver. There was no doubt about it that I had a thing for him, even though he was something like family to me. He held me tight and kissed me on the forehead. I accidentally moaned and stood up on my tippy-toes to feel his lips better. I wrapped my arms around him, then trailed them around to his front and squeezed his rock-hard chest and stomach. It felt like he was packing concrete under there.

I looked up at him and lightly kissed his lips, licking them in the process. He grabbed me by both arms and held me out in front of him, giving me a look that said I must have lost my mind. I wiggled out of his grip and hugged him again. Reaching between us, I grabbed his dick through his pants. It felt like I had trapped a cucumber. I felt it throb, and that drove me crazy.

He reached down and grabbed my wrist. "Ariana, what the fuck are you doing? You already know you're my family. You're like my little daughter. I can't go there with you like that." He tried to pry my hands from around him.

"Then fuck me, daddy. Fuck your baby and make me feel all better. I promise I won't tell nobody, I just need you inside of me to show me your love." I reached, grabbed his hand, and put it in my panties and spread my legs wide.

To my surprise, he didn't move his hand out of there right away.

"You feel that, daddy? Huh? Do you feel how hot your little girl is for you right now? Since day one I been needing you, daddy."

I felt his fingers moving around inside of my panties. He spread my lips and slid a finger up my box. I moaned and stood on my tippy-toes as I felt his digit moving in and out of me. I leaned forward and sucked on his neck, and he picked me up and sat me on the table with my legs wide open.

"Damn, you like my daughter, though. I hope this shit don't feel weird." He dropped down, yanked my panties to the side, and began slurping on my jewel as if it were raw oysters.

I spread my legs wide while he ate and said so many curse words I was sure I needed to pray afterward. I had never had my pussy eaten so perfectly and so nastily. He knew all the right spots to hit and what to do with my button down there. I came four times in less than 10 minutes, screaming out for him and calling him Daddy. It seemed like every time he heard me call him that, he'd suck my jewel even harder and make me come again.

He took a step back and dropped his jeans. I almost broke my neck dropping to my knees. When I saw his penis, I nearly came again.

It was so thick and big, full of veins. The head looked like the top of the Arby's symbol. I sucked him into my mouth, and all the way to the back of my throat again and again.

That didn't last long before he picked me up and bent me over the chair in the kitchen, positioned himself at my box, and slammed forward with so much power I came again.

He held my hips and fucked me into a woman. I say that because I had never been fucked so good and so perfectly hard. I fell in love right away, especially when he picked me up and fucked me up against the refrigerator while he told me how good my pussy was. Then he fell to the floor with me and long-stroked me while I bit all over his chest and put scratches on his back. He dug me out, and I loved every minute of it.

After we finished, I promised I would not say anything, and I meant that. There was no way I was about to lose access to his dick. I already found myself following him around the house and sniffing the air. I was obsessed, and I knew it.

***

That night we got another Facetime message from Alexis. As soon as my phone vibrated, I recognized the number. I accepted it, and her face came onto the screen.

"Mom! Hurry, come here! Alexis is on my phone."

I heard every door in the house opening up, and the sound of a bunch of feet on the floor in a hurry. My mother ran into the room and snatched the phone away from me so fast I didn't even feel her do it. I felt a little jealous, but that only lasted for a fleeting moment. I knew she missed my sister, and she needed to know she was alive and well. She had been lying around the house in a major state of depression every since she got there. I had not been able to experience the real her because of the situation we found ourselves in.

***

Tiny

"Alexis, baby, talk to me. Are you okay?" I asked, praying silently to God she was. I could not hear anything other than my heart beating inside of my chest. I felt my blood pressure rising. Things got a little blurry. I tried to shake the cobwebs out of my head. She was saying something, but I could not focus my hearing.

"Mom, I'm okay." Tears fell down her cheeks. "I'm scared, though, Mommy, and I don't know what to do. When are you corning to get me away from here?" Snot ran out of her nose. She wiped it away with her hand and swallowed. I could see her chest heaving up and down as if she was starting to become hysterical.

"Calm down, baby." Tears were all over my face now. "I promise you I will be there to save you soon. You know I would never leave you nor forsake you. I love you way too much for that." I wished I could have held her right then. Since my child had been alive, I had never gotten the chance to hold her or to feed her. I wanted to tend to her needs. I wanted to make her happy and to protect her. My baby needed me, and I felt like I should have been able to save her on day one.

" Morn, I'm losing my mind here. He keeps me in some type of bedroom in a dungeon all day long. I don't know where I am. All I know is I have to get out of here pretty fast or I'm going to take my own life."

She broke down into a fit of coughs while she cried. I saw her head jerk backward, and the next thing I knew Jaheim stuck his face into the camera.

"Well, hello there, everybody. It's certainly a bright and shiny day, am I right?" He leaned down and kissed Alexis on the cheek, sucking her jaw into his mouth and letting it go. "I can never get enough of all this chocolate. Mm!"

"Jaheim, get your fucking hands off of my daughter, you sick fucking pervert!" I screamed and almost threw the phone against the wall. I hated seeing him touch my daughter in any way. Every time he touched her, it made me want to kill the closest person to me. I felt my blood go red hot. I could not wait to get him back. I would never be able to sleep at night until I knew my daughter was safe and sound and Jaheim has suffered the worst fate known to man.

"Pervert? Wow. Now, that's not any way to talk to the person who can literally cut your daughter's fucking head off, is it?" At that, he left and appeared back in focus with a machete. "I will cut this pretty bitch's head off if you ever disrespect me like that again. Don't you know who you're fucking with?" He pulled Alexis by her hair and exposed her throat. "Now, say you're sorry." He turned his head sideways.

"I'm sorry, Jaheim. I'm sorry. I will never disrespect you like that again." I wanted to kill him ten times worse now. How dare he cause my child great harm and then make me apologize to him? This fool had some nerve. "Look at you being all polite and shit. I guess I can accept your apology, since you're trying to be the bigger man." He took the machete away from Alexis' throat and licked her face from the chin to her forehead. "Now, I want everybody in that room where you are to squeeze into the camera and bow down and apologize to me just because all y'all are a bunch of sorry muthafuckas. Do it now, and hurry the fuck up!" he demanded, placing the blade back to Alexis' throat.

One-by-one, we bowed down and squeezed together with Roman in the middle and apologized. This man had lost his mind. I wondered if he was doped up off of some form of drug. I couldn't really see his eyes that clearly, but I could only imagine. Back in the day, he had a serious addiction to cocaine and heroin. I didn't think people like him just kicked the habit.

"Alright, get up now, and y'all tell me how close are you to having my money? The clock is ticking, you know. We're down to seven days after today." He pulled Alexis up, sat in the chair she was sitting in, and made her sit in his lap.

"We'll have the money, you can believe that. Just don't hurt my little girl," I begged. I could hear sniffling in the room behind me. I knew everybody was probably crying. This whole ordeal made no sense. No family should ever have to deal with the scenario that we were.

"You see, I didn't ask you if you would have it. What I asked you is how close are you to having it? How much do you have right now? Come on, tell me!" He reached in front of him and placed his hands under Alexis' shirt.

Roman spoke up. "Yo, we got 300 thousand right now, and I'll have the rest by the deadline." He curled his upper lip and clenched his jaw off and on. "My question is if we can get this paper to you sooner than the date you asked, will you release her safe and sound?"

"Nigga, who the fuck is you?" Jaheim asked and began sucking on Alexis' neck.

"Yo, that's my li'l cousin right there, and she's my world. I'm trying to make sure she's released as soon as possible, and safe."

At saying the last part, I could see him adjust the gun on his waist. He was heated, and if he could have killed Jaheim right there, I knew it would have been a bloodbath.

Jaheim laughed. "Oh, so you're the cousin, huh? I guess you're supposed to be their li'l savior and shit." He laughed and pulled up Alexis' shirt, exposing her bare chest underneath. "Let me ask you something, cuz: have you ever seen any titties that were as perfect as these?"

Roman turned his face away from the camera and covered his eyes. "Yo, I ain't trying to see my li'l cousin's shit like that, homie. Why don't you get off that dumb shit and let's handle this business as men. We can leave these women out of this." Roman continued to not look into the live feed.

"Nigga, look at me when you're talking to me. I want you to watch this shit and answer my question, or I'm gon' cut this li'l bitch's head *off*!" He screamed the word 'off' as if he was starting to lose his patience. "Look at her!"

Roman turned back to the camera and looked into it. "Alright, man, now I'm looking. Can we please move on from this? Let's talk business." He clenched his jaw off and on, faster and faster. I saw him also wrap his hand around the handle of his pistol.

"Answer my question," Jaheim demanded.

Roman took a deep breath and blew out the air. "What is your question, homie?"

"My question was have you ever seen a pair of titties this pretty or as perfect as these?"

Roman lowered his head. I could only imagine what was taking place in his mind. How was he supposed to answer the question without looking some type of way? I didn't know what I would have done or said if I had been in his shoes, but I did know in the end he would get Jaheim back for this humiliation of himself and Alexis.

"You know what, Jaheim? My li'l cousin is perfect, and I will never lay my eyes on anybody more perfect than her. So nall, I ain't never seen none better."

Jaheim smirked. "Ain't you just the sweetest bitch-nigga I ever met before. Your pussy probably fatter than hers, ain't it?" He laughed at his own joke. "But, nall, on some real shit, though, I want that 300 gees by tomorrow. I'm gon' have one of my connects meet up with you, playboy. Make sure you have them numbers right or there's going to be trouble. I can assure you of that shit."

Roman shook his head. "Nall, that ain't gon' work. I need until Monday morning, first thing."

"But you just said you had 300 bands ready for me right now, so why am I waiting until then?" He put the blade back to Alexis' throat. "Sounds like some bullshit in the air to me. You better explain yourself right the fuck now!"

Roman mugged the camera. "That's when my paper will be right, so that's when I'll have your bread. Ain't shit moving until then. That's just the way it is."

"Ah yeah, that's how you feel? Then how about I just stank this bitch right now and be done with this shit?" he threatened.

Roman flared his nostrils and didn't give him a response.

Now I was starting to panic. I felt my cousin's temper was getting the better of him, and he was about to snap. I had seen the look on his face a hundred times before, and I knew it meant he was ready to go ballistic.

"Hey, Jaheim, just let us hit your hand on Monday morning. That way everybody will be good. Now, if we give you all of that, what insurance do we have that we will get her and everything will be on the up-and-up?" I started shaking because I was already anticipating his response.

"Insurance? Bitch, this ain't All State!" He laugh and placed his hands back under Alexis' shirt and began moving them around. "I might be a dirty nigga, but I ain't that damn dirty. You see, I just want the money. I couldn't care less about this li'l fox. Now, don't get me wrong, she sure is fine and all, but she ain't $500,000 fine! Y'all get me my money, and I'll get you your bitch. It's as simple as that."

I didn't trust this dude as far as I could throw him, and he had gained some weight since I saw him last, so I definitely could not throw him far. I just felt like something was up with him. I wished I knew where my baby was being kept. I'd say fuck the money and risk running up in there with guns blazing.

"Alright then, homie. I'll have your bread by 8:00 a.m. Monday morning, no later." Roman nodded his head.

"Well, it seems like that's that, then. Y'all have my paper Monday and everything should flow smoothly. All you'll owe me then is 200 stacks." He looked down at Alexis. "I personally don't think she's worth all of that, but then again, I ain't the dumb muthafuckas paying for her ransom. Y'all wanna say something to her before we go? I'm thinking I might take her virginity tonight. I don't know yet." He laughed with his head tilted backward.

"Alexis, baby, I love you, and we're coming for you. Do you understand that?" I had tears rolling down my cheeks. My entire shirt was wet. I could feel it sticking to my chest.

"Yes, Momma, I hear you. And I love you, too. Please don't forget about me, and please get to me as soon as possible. I hate it here. " She cried with her mouth wide open.

"Keep your head up, li'l momma. You already know I got you, and I love you, Boo-Boo. I'm gon' get this bread together so we can get you home. Mind over matter, don't you forget that. And when you get here, I'm gon' spoil your ass to death, that's my word." For the first time I saw tears in Roman's eyes.

"I love you, too, Roman, and I know you got me. I don't have any doubt in my mind. Just get to me as soon as you can, please."

"I love you, too, sis, and I'm trying to do my part as well. Please keep fighting, and you will be here in no time, that's for sure. We will never stop fighting for you. Never!"

Ariana ran to Roman, and he wrapped his arms around her as she cried hysterical.

Jackie got onto the phone and waved. "Hey, girl. I'm here for you as well, and anything I can do for you, I absolutely will. You are in my heart and in my soul. I know first-hand you are a fighter, so fight." She gave her the peace sign and blew her a kiss.

Lastly, Leah came to the phone's camera and waved. "I miss you. I am going crazy without you, but I stay under our morn 24/7. I love you through her until you get back here. Please be strong, because we all need you."

Jaheim snatched the phone away. "Alright, enough with all that mushy shit! Have my paper. I'll be in touch."

With that, the screen faded to black.

Chapter 9

Roman

After the whole thing with this Jaheim rat, I was red-hot. I was so mad I could barely see straight. The only thing on my mind was death. Every time I blinked, all I saw on the back of my eyelids was that nigga laying in a coffin with his face disfigured. I could not believe this stud had the audacity to pull the ho-shit he did, playing around with my li'l cousin like everything was a game. Who did he think he was?

I looked at my dashboard as I swerved in and out of traffic. I was going over 80 miles an hour, even flying through stop signs as if they didn't mean nothing. I had to calm down, because if I didn't, my li'l cousin would be ass-out. She needed me to get that paper. I was her only hope.

I rang the doorbell to Emily's parents' big mansion and waited as patiently as I could. I had to keep rolling my head around on my neck because my temper was blazing. There seemed to be a whole lot of mosquitoes out that night. They kept flying all into my face and crawling along the back of my neck. I had popped so many by the time her butler answered the door that I seriously wanted to pop his ass.

I ran straight up the spiral staircase and down the hall, headed for her room when she came out of it and met me halfway. She looked as if she was shocked to see me. I walked right past her, went into her room, and sat on the bed. "What's good?"

She closed her bedroom door and laid her back up against it as if she didn't know what to say. "Roman, I wasn't expecting you to come." She came and sat on the bed beside me and tried to put my arm around her shoulder.

I yanked my arm away and stood up. "Yo, why you acting like you don't know what I'm here for?" I frowned, ready to beat her li'l white ass. I didn't have time to be playing no games. I needed to see if she had this money in order for me, or else I had to follow my plan B and C.

She looked nervous, biting her fingernail and chewing on her bottom lip. "Babe, I told you I would be in touch when I had my hands on everything. I haven't managed to get that amount as of yet, but I am trying."

She tried to get up and hug me. I pushed her away and sidestepped her all together on my way out the door when she ran in front of it.

"Please, Roman, just hear me out."

"Get the fuck away from the door, Emily. I got business to take care of. I gotta make shit happen, because clearly I can't depend on you." I shook my head. "You always talking about you wanna be my li'l white bitch and all that, and you can't even handle the simple task of checking your people's accounts for me." I wrapped her nightgown into my fist and pulled her away from the door.

She had the nerve to jump onto my back. "Please, Roman, it's not like that's a small sum of money. That's a lot. I am trying to do everything I can short of sleeping with my own father to make it happen for you. I just need a day or two and you'll have your money." She said this through tears.

"In a day or two, my li'l cousin could be dead. I only have until Sunday night to have the cash. After midnight they are going to kill her. I cannot allow that to happen.

Now, get off my fucking back, because all you're doing is stopping my progress."

She held onto me tighter. "No, please, Roman, I need you. You're my black hood blessing. I need all of your ebony essence. You can't go away from me, please." She started to kiss my bald head. "Hey, I'll tell you what. I can get you 50 thousand by the morning, and you can also have my Mercedes Roadster and the Tesla Roadster. You should be able to get at least 250 grand from those cars alone. Then I'll do whatever I have to in order to get the rest of the money. Just don't leave me, please!"

***

I beat on the door to my trap house, and Cavali answered it wearing a bulletproof vest. I gave him a half-hug and shook up with him.

Walking past him, I saw the spot was in full effect. It was jam-packed with so much dope in the air I had to put my mask on. They had a table out so long it looked like it was used to have the whole neighborhood sit down at once to eat. But that wasn't the case for this table. This table had 10 workers on each side, chopping and bagging dope. The first side would chop and weigh the right amount and slide it across the table to the one who was supposed to bag it. The operation looked smooth, just the way I had trained them.

In the kitchen there were two electric stoves going, and my man Chef was running both of them with the good-white being mixed and whipped in the rawest fashion. He saw me and gave me a nod. I returned it and walked past him and down the basement steps. As soon as I got to the bottom, I heard the sound of steel. I came all the way down the steps and saw there were so many guns laid out I would have sworn we were about to go to war with the President. There were about twenty masked young men in the room loading up all kinds of firearms. To this sight I simply nodded my head. I was in a murderous mood and ready to move on them fools up the block. I wanted to get some blood on my hands just so I could feel better.

Cavali came up beside me and put his hand on my shoulder. "You ready to take a good look at these niggas or what? Because I definitely am." He walked over and picked up an AR-15, tapped the trigger, prompting a green beam to appear. "This gon' be my baby, right here. I'm gon' finger-fuck her so good she gon' spit and spit again." He rubbed the gun against his face and licked the barrel.

Now, this was the kind of shit I loved, but was also trying to get away from. It was so hard to leave that kind of life behind, though, no matter what I tried. I picked up a mini AK-47 and a .44 Desert Eagle with the extended clip. I loved DEs. They were so accurate, and they blew a head clean off. I was about to screw somebody over, and I wasn't worrying about wearing a rubber this time.

I sat everybody down and explained to them what our mission was going to be. Every last soldier in the room I had snatched up out of the projects after their parents went down under King's spell. I trusted them to a point, and I knew I had to put my faith in them in order to accomplish this next task of business.

I calculated in my head that the house down the way had to be holding about $400,000.00 in it with everything included.

That's money and street value of the dope. The house also held heroin and cocaine. They were just starting to venture out into the pill scene, but I didn't know how established they were, so I didn't project any real numbers from that.

Now, I had a vast knowledge of the fool who ran the operation because we both had come up under Draylon. His name was Valentino, but the hood called him V. He also had a right-hand man named Moan. Both had grown up with me, but we weren't friends. Quiet as I kept, I didn't like either one of the niggas. I barely like dudes, period, but them two just weren't my cup of tea, mostly because I looked at them as competition, and also because, well, I just didn't like them, so it was time to move on them.

***

The next night, me and Cavali were parked outside of Anila's daycare center. We had been watching Valentino's wife the whole night, tracking her movements. This had to be the last stop on her list of tasks. At least, that's what Cavali told me. He had been tracking her for the last five days and told me this was her normal routine.

She went inside and came back out holding the hand of a little boy who kept trying to dance and do the dab move. She seemed to be getting angry and a little frustrated. The sun was just beginning to go down, and the night was extremely humid. I kept the AC on because I was having a hard time breathing. The air was so thick it seemed like I could cut it with a knife.

She loaded the little boy into her Hyundai Genesis, and we followed close behind.

"Yo, I really don't like bagging women, bruh, but sometimes shit happens," Cavali said, cocking back his pistol.

I wasn't really the type to body females either. I felt drama between men was supposed to stay between them, women and kids should never be the target. I hadn't ever put a bullet in a woman before. I mean, I came close. One time a female upped a gun on me and pulled the trigger twice, aiming at my head, but her gun still had the safety on. What's crazy about that situation was I was letting her go. As soon as I thought she was out of sight, I finished stripping her man. No more than 30 seconds later, she came back around the corner, squeezing the trigger straight in my face. Had she known how to use the safety, I would have been a dead man. That broad caught two to the shoulder and lost both of her kneecaps. Her man, on the other hand… well, let's just say he didn't fair so well.

"Hopefully we ain't gotta body this broad, though. Her only purpose is to get us into the house, and open that safe. We gon' tie her ass up and go from there. Nothing else makes any sense."

Cavali laughed. "Yo, I ain't saying I won't body her. Just ain't my cup of tea." He rubbed his hand over his chest and adjusted his vest some. "What kind of security you think they got? "

Up ahead, the car turned into the drive-thru of Chubby Burger, and I got a little irritated because she was going off course. I wanted to bust this move and be over and done with it. I needed to see this paper in my hands. As soon as she opened the safe, I'd be able to give the go ahead for our troops to proceed with part two of the mission.

Loyal to the Game 3

"I ain't never seen this broad do this before. She must be tired and don't feel like cooking." He shook his head and sank lower in his seat. "What we gon' do, bro? Because we can't follow her through the drive-thru and then expect her not to notice us following her all the way home. Besides, there is a camera recording all of that." He looked pissed and super impatient.

I started to mull things over in my head. Time was money, and we needed everything to flow properly. There wasn't much of a line at Chubby Burger, so I decided to let her do what she do. I ducked off on the side street directly across from where the place was located. I waited for her to finish her business, and then we continued to follow her all they way to her house she shared with Valentino.

Chapter 10

Ariana

I nearly jumped out of my skin as I was crossing the street coming from the gas station and a pink Jeep screeched on its brakes and rolled down the window. I just knew Noah had hired somebody to kill me. He had already sent a few people at me who came out of the blue with offers, none of them worth my time, but it was the fact they kept on jumping out at me in random places that let me know Noah could touch me if he really wanted to.

I closed my eyes and prepared myself for the impact of bullets. I already imagined an angel was coming to take away my soul. Maybe it would drop me off where my mother was, or maybe I'd become one of them myself. No matter what took place, I just prayed it didn't hurt.

I stood there like a damn fool until I heard my name coming out of a female's voice box.

"Ariana! Girl, if you don't get your stupid-ass out of the street, I'm gon' hit you with my truck!" the familiar voice commanded. I opened my eyes to see Rosie waving at me out of her Jeep's window.

Rosie was my sister's best friend. They grew up together and did everything together. When we first found out something had happened to Alexis, Rosie was down in Mexico visiting her relatives. I chatted with her on Facebook and saw how she broke down. She promised me when she got back in town she would hit me up and do whatever she could to help out with my sister.

I slid into her passenger seat, leaned over, and gave her a hug. "What's good ,girl? When did you get back into town?" I adjusted my seat because it was pushed all the way back like before me a dude had been sitting in my place. Her car smelled like she had just come from a restaurant.

"I just got back in town today, and I was on my way to your fine-ass cousin's house. I wanted to surprise you and see Alexis' mom for the first time." She pulled back into traffic, using her turn signal. "I also wouldn't mind seeing Roman, either." She ran her tongue across her lips. "Have you heard anything else from Alexis?"

I was trying to focus on what she was asking me, but a major part of me was still stuck on what she'd said about Roman. I mean, I got jealous immediately. This bitch was bad with her long, straight black hair and her urban porn star body. I got to feeling insecure right away, like I ain't even want her to go to the house.

"Girl, did you hear what I asked you?"

I had to shake my head to tune into what she was saying.

My mind had completely drifted off, then I started to feel some type of way because she was inquiring about my sister. I had to get ahold of my emotions. I had to understand Roman was not my man. It just sucked he put the dick on me the way he did. It was so bad I found myself fien'ing for it.

"Yeah. Oh, um, we heard from her last night, and that dude was demanding a whole bunch of money from us by Monday. He was live-chatting with us and feeling all over Alexis. It was so unbearable to watch."

Rosie shook her head slowly. "That sucks. I mean, who is this guy, anyway?" She made a right turn and nearly clipped another car. She yelled out something in Spanish and waved her fist at the driver. I thought she was out of her mind. She must not have known people in

Chicago were still crazy and would kill a person at the drop of a hat.

I didn't want to tell her the man that had Alexis was my biological father because I didn't know how to address that fact. I mean, no one in the house did. I never understood how nobody brought it up. Every time I saw his face on the screen, I looked at him for facial similarities within myself. I know he was my sister's captor, but I still had a yearning within to see as much of him as possible. I didn't want to be with him, I just found a major part of me was curious as to who he was. Now, I know that may sound weird, but my whole life I was raised inside of a foster home. I never had the chance to see my mother or any side of her family, so a part of me has always grown up wishing I knew who I really was. Even though he was a monster, a part of me yearned to understand him as a man.

"Can I be honest with you about something, Rosie, without you freaking out or judging me?" I turned to her to gauge her more closely. I didn't really know her too well, but I figured if my sister really cared about her and they kicked it together every day, they must have had a lot in common. And according to all of those people I was currently living with who had actually lived with my sister, Alexis was known to be a very down-to-earth, non-judgmental person with a good heart.

She glanced over at me for a few seconds, then turned back to the road. "Yeah, sure, sis. You can tell me anything. I won't judge you or get mad, at least I'll try not to." she smiled weakly, reached and squeezed my thigh playfully.

"Okay, well, here goes nothing." I sighed out loud. "The man that has Alexis is my biological father. He, my mother, and Alexis' mother used to work the streets together, or they worked the streets for him. Before Alexis was born, her mother was pregnant with another child Jaheim beat out of her. My mother was also pregnant by him at the same time. Long story short, he's my father, and nobody even talks about that fact in the house. Sometimes it just feels weird being there while all of this stuff is going on. I feel like it's my fault, especially since he keeps on saying he took Alexis away because her mother took me away from him."

Rosie raised her left eyebrow. "Did she?"

"No, he never wanted me to begin with, and neither did my mother. That's why she gave me up and killed herself. Nobody has ever wanted me, and I have always felt so alone." By this time I was bawling. I could not catch my breath.

Rosie pulled the Jeep over and hugged me. "Everything will work itself out, Ariana. You have to believe that and know it to be true. Now we're going to find a way to help Alexis back together. All we need to do is sit down and put our brains together. Nothing or no one is smarter than the female species. We have it in us to get things done."

She rubbed my back and pressed my head onto her shoulder more firmly just as a bum came up and knocked on the window, scaring both of us half to death. He took a spray bottle and began to wash the windows, wiping them down with some dirty newspaper. He knocked on the passenger window and directed us to roll it down by motioning his hands. He was bald with an incredibly long white beard that was turning brown. It looked like he'd been drinking liquor for the last five years and spilled a lot of it right onto his beard.

We tried to shoo him away, but he simply sprayed the passenger's window and wiped it down, also. Behind him, standing on the sidewalk was a slim female with pink rollers in her hair, digging in her nose. She pulled something out and wiped it on the bottom of her shoe.

Rosie waved him off again. "Hey, *vato*, get the hell out of here! *Ve*! We didn't ask you to do that," she said, yelling over my shoulder.

He put his hand to his ear as if he couldn't hear her. We could hear him through the glass perfectly fine. "I can't hear you, little lady. Roll your window down."

The sun shined off his yellow face. He teeth were mostly gone, and the ones that were there looked like a wooden picket fence.

Rosie got irritated and stepped out of the vehicle. She walked around the Jeep and stood directly in front of him, only then did I roll my window down so I could hear. He laughed, and opened his arms as if expecting a hug.

"Look, man, I didn't ask you to touch my shit. Now get the fuck out of here. I'm not paying you a dime." She turned to walk back to the car, but the street was full of oncoming traffic.

"You mean to tell me I just worked eight hours washing and fixing your car and you just gon' do me like that? Oh no, baby girl, now that ain't right." He started to cry. "All my life I had to fight, but I never thought I had to fight at work. I almost got kicked my that old mule." He started doing drunken steps of karate, then fell down, hitting the splits with his hands together like he was praying.

Rosie turned to him and shook her head. "You silly fool, that's why I'm not giving you a dollar, because you're already out of your freaking mind." She looked over at the woman who stood a safe distance away, holding onto the shopping cart filled with cans. She had her finger up her nose again with her eyes closed.

"I need the money to buy a house. I gotta get out of this snow. It's freezing out here. He fanned his face, and blocked his eyes from the sun. In one quick motion, he hopped up and ran into the street, nearly getting hit by a car. Then he ran back over and hopped onto Rosie's hood of her Jeep, spraying the windshield.

Rosie snapped, "Get the fuck off of my shit, you dirty-ass nigga. I ain't giving you a dime. I'm hip to your tricks, so you won't get a crumb from me, you can bet your ass on that." She stood on the bumper and pulled on his shirt to free him from her Jeep.

He smacked her hand away and sprayed more of the fluid onto her windshield. "I been working here since I was a kid. How you gon' close this factory now? What are we supposed to do? Where are we supposed to go? I got a whole family to feed, especially momma." His bottom lip began to quiver. "Ever since the accident she ain't been the same. She just ain't been the same!" He waved his hand through the air. "But that's okay because He supplies all of my needs. He supplies all of my needs, woo, woo, woo," he sang, waving his hand through the air as if he were in church.

Rosie got all the way on the hood with him and kicked him square in the ribs. He fell off the hood and did a boxing stance, jumped, did a back flip, and screamed at the top of his lungs that he was Muhammad Ali.

I was trying my best to not bust out laughing, but this dude was a trip. I mean, I could not believe how much he had going on in that head. And then another thing, he looked to be about 60, and he was moving around like a

20-year-old, hitting flips and all kinds of stuff. I found him amusing.

Rosie took her big hoop earrings off and put up her guard. "Oh, you want some drama, old man? *Sabes que,* then let's go." She stepped forward and punched him straight in the nose, ducked, and smacked him with an open hand. "That's how we do it on the south side, fool. What's good?" She bounced on her toes, took her thumb, and rubbed the side of her nose with it.

When she hit him, he yelped and did a cartwheel. "Whew-wee, they got me back in Vietnam. Well, I gotta fight for my country." He dug into his pants and came up with a pair of nun chucks. "I told you this was a secret mission, but there you go, cheating in the next room." He worked the weapon all around his body, and gave her a look that said he was serious.

Rosie, clearly not one to back down, took her belt from around her waist and wrapped it around her right hand, leaving the buckle hanging. It was a big buckle, too. Looked like a gold lunch box or something. She ran at him and whacked him with it. He tried to run and fell, so she hit him with it again and kicked him in the butt with her Jordans. "Get the fuck out of here, you clown!"

The man took off, running with the woman behind him, pushing the shopping cart so fast she tripped a few times trying to keep up. We saw him jump onto another car about a half a block down. I shook my head as Rosie got back into her Jeep.

"These muthafuckas out here are just crazy. Everybody seems to be geeked up on something, but I ain't backing down. Fuck that. I refuse to be a *chochita.*" She pulled out into traffic just as the sun completely disappeared. We didn't get more than two blocks before a red Benz truck got behind us and flashed its high beams. She looked into the rearview mirror and smiled. "Oh, shit, that's my man, right there. That's Chris. Oh, shit, I can't believe it."

She pulled up to the red light and he pulled alongside of us. She rolled down the window. "Hey, *papi*, what you doing?"

He rolled down his passenger window and began to yell out of it, even though he had a female sitting in it. "Yo, what's good, Rosie?" The female he was hollering over looked so uncomfortable, but he didn't seem to pay it any mind at all. He leaned further out of her side of the window and motioned for her to pull over, and we did.

"You know he's been to our house already, right?" I didn't really know what their relation was to one another because I previously thought Chris was Alexis' old boyfriend, so I was a bit confused.

Rosie rolled down her window as he walked up to it. "Who is that bitch you got rolling with you?" she asked, not wasting any time at all. She flipped her long hair over her shoulders and licked her thick lips. I could not help but admit she was extremely attractive.

"Oh, that's just some bitch I picked up from the plaza. She topped me off, now I'm about to drop her back off on the east side." He looked past her and nodded in a *what up* fashion to me. I returned his nod and sat back more firm in my seat.

Rosie reached through the window and grabbed him by his shirt, a playful, yet menacing smile on her face. "Nigga, you out there fucking hos and playing in the streets when my sister is missing?" She tightened her grip. "Don't you know she went out of town with your homeboy, and that's one of the reasons she's missing right now?" She flared her nostrils.

Chris laughed and smacked at her hand. "Shorty, if you don't let my muthafuckin' shit go, we about to have a problem."

Cars whipped by him in the background. I looked over his shoulder and saw a stray dog trying to cross the street. Rosie let him go and sat back in her seat. He leaned into the window, and they made out super loud. He slid his hand inside her blouse and pulled most of her breast out. I could make out one full nipple, big, brown, and erect. At first I felt a little uneasy, but when I saw that I couldn't help rubbing my thighs together, and I was starting to get a little saucy down there.

They broke the embrace and Chris looked over at me and smiled. "Yo, once we figure this whole thing out and get Alexis back, I'm trying to take both of y'all to the Bahamas where we can get as nasty as hell. I wanna see you too fuck each other, and then I'm gon' dick both of y'all down while we overlook the ocean. How that sound?"

I couldn't help blushing. All of that sounded good to me because he was damn sure fine. He had money and a nice swag about himself. I would be game, plus I was feeling Rosie low-key anyway.

"Long as you're paying and you throw in a crazy shopping spree, I'll fuck you and her wherever. Besides, what's one man between two sisters?" She licked her lips, reached over, and ran her hand all the way up my thigh, in between my legs, and cupped my kitty. I jumped from the contact. "Nothing but fun, am I right?"

I felt her hand moving under my short skirt and embarrassed myself because I knew my panties were getting wet.

Chris could not take his eyes off her wandering hand. "Yo, it ain't tricking if you got a whole lot of it, so I'm game. I got some shit to run by you and Ms. Johnson. We need to make this happen for your homegirl and my mans, so I'll be in touch real soon." He reached into his pocket and came up with a knot of cash. He pulled her blouse back along with her bra, exposing the big, brown nipple to my eyes. He then placed the knot inside of her bra and kissed her cheek. "This about 10 gees worth of pocket change for you. Buy you and her something nice."

Chapter 11

Roman

We wound up beating her there and waiting on the side of the house for her. I wanted to make things go as easy as possible, and if I could avoid hurting her and the kid, then that would be great. My main concern, though, was the money and getting it as quickly as possible. We didn't have time to play no games, and I wasn't about to.

They stayed in a big middle class, all white house with a white picket fence around it. It looked like the garage was big enough to fit two cars inside of it. Even though it was nighttime, I could tell the lawn was freshly mown, and overall it looked like a nice duck off.

I always found it crazy the majority of our people thought it was cool to sell drugs and tear up where we were raised and brought up, and when they reached any kind of success at all, they left and went to another neighborhood where they had no roots. There they tried to be on their best behavior and, most times, did all they could to feed and uplift that community while they kept going back to their homeland and adding to the disaster.

I waited until she pulled her car into the garage and got out. She opened the back door and allowed the child to exit the car as well. I was trying to figure out how we would snatch them up without the kid screaming or her doing the same, causing a scene. They both had to be snatched at the same time or there was going to be a problem.

As soon as the boy got out of the car, she bent down to pick him up. He looked to be a little tired, because she was trying to get him to walk on his own, but that wasn't happening. I saw him stand outside of the back door to the car and stomp his little feel. She let out a sigh and seemed as if she were very annoyed by his behavior.

"Listen, I cannot carry you and the food in the house at the same time. Now, you're two years old. You can walk."

He jumped up and down and plopped down on the pavement. She grabbed him by his arm and flung him over her shoulder.

My eyes got as big as saucers. I thought she was going to slam him down or something. It was amazing what parents did when they thought nobody else was watching. She tried to grab the bags out of the back of the car, but could not because he was flopping around like he was crazy. A part of me felt sorry for her. She made me realize how hard women really had it from time to time as a mother.

I guess she must have decided against trying to carry the groceries into the house, because she placed him on her hip and opened the inside of the garage door that led into the house. When she disappeared, I dive into the backseat of the car while Cavali hid behind a rack of mountain bikes. He looked like a big-ass blob of ink in all his black, trying to squeeze into that tight space.

I heard her coming back. She opened the door to the car, causing the interior light to come on. As soon as it did, I pressed the .44 Magnum to her forehead and told her if she screamed, I would splatter her in her garage. "Do you understand that? Nod your head if you do."

She did.

Very slowly, I climbed out of the backseat, holding the gun to her forehead. She was a nice redbone female with long, curly hair and a beautiful face. I had not seen her in the hood, which meant Valentino kept her in the house, and I could understand that 100 percent. See, for a lady, if she has a man that desires to keep her inside the house all the time and away from the hood, that just means he sees a wife in her. Men, hustlers in general that are having cash, always like to duck off what's special to them. They like to stash things away that are of value. We keep the baddest woman we're involved with in the best possible position and environment. If a lady has a man who always keeps her inside of the hood or hasn't changed her surrounding for the better, then they're either fucking with a loser or a man who already has his treasure tucked safely away, and he does not see worth in her.

"Check this out, shorty. We gon' go in this house, and you're going to open that safe, and I'm gon' leave back out of here without killing nobody. However, if we go in this house and you start playing games with me, then there will be bloodshed. I can promise you that." I grabbed her by her hair and led her into the kitchen, the first place the garage door led. "Let's go!" I said, yanking her hair a little bit for dramatic effect.

"Okay, please just don't hurt me."

As soon as we entered the house, the little boy was sitting on the floor in front of the refrigerator with his whole hand inside of a birthday cake. He didn't even pay us any mind. His entire face was covered in frosting. I almost laughed because it was so funny to me.

When he saw us, he started apologizing. "I'm sowee, Mommy. I sowee!"

He got up and hugged his mother's legs, then ran out of the kitchen, leaving the cake where it was. I kicked it to the side and closed the door to the refrigerator.

"Say, li'l one, how many more people are in this house?" I asked, walking us very slowly out of the kitchen. The kitchen led right into the dining room where an long oak table sat already made up with china plates and utensils. There was a ceiling fan spinning, and to my left was a big, flat plasma TV.

I didn't know which way the boy had went, but the last thing I needed was for him to jump out of nowhere and scare me so bad I popped him. I wasn't into killing kids under no circumstances, not even this one.

"There is no one else here. It's just me and my son. Please, don't hurt us. I am begging you with all that I am."

"Yeah, well, all you gotta do is tell me where the safe is and I'll be out of your hair." I pushed her forward. "Where is it? Lead me, and I'll follow you."

She pointed forward toward the steps. I heard the little boy playing somewhere in the distance, but I couldn't make out where.

I saw a movement to my right in the shadows and aimed my weapon at it, ready to bust, until I saw it was Cavali. He nodded at me and put a finger to his lips.

She led me up the stairs and down the hall toward their bedroom. On the way, we passed the little boy's room, and I heard him in there on a tablet. I peeked in and saw he was dancing to whatever image was on the screen.

When we got all the way down the long hallway, we opened the door to her and Valentino's bedroom. As soon as we got there, I pushed her in and she fell on the bed. I closed the door behind us and pointed the gun directly at her. "Shorty, let's get this show on the road. Where the fuck is the safe?" I pulled her up and threw her toward the closet. She fell down and tried to get back up.

"It's in the closet. Please, just calm down and I'll get it for you. I don't want any trouble." She climbed to her feet and pulled back the folding doors on the closet. Pushing all of her clothes that were on hangers out of the way, she cleared a space and knelt down.

I stepped up and put the gun to the back of her head. "What the fuck are you doing?" I looked around the room for cameras, recording devices, or anything. I even looked to see if her laptop that was sitting on the dresser had a camera on it, and it did. I reached and closed the screen.

"Calm down, the safe is right in this trap here. She twisted a latch and the wall opened up. Once it did, a digital face appeared with button that were lit up green. She paused and looked it over for a second, and that's when we heard her son yell for her.

She jumped up and proceeded to run to the door. I tackled her. "What the fuck are you doing? Get your ass back over there and open that safe!" I flung her toward the closet and blocked her way to the door. We had already been in there too long. I was ready to leave.

The little boy was all of the sudden deadly quiet.

"Let me go and get my son! Please, what if something happens to him?"

She ran for the door again, and once more I threw her on the floor, tired of her antics.

"I'm not doing shit unless you allow me to go and get my son! I mean it." She had tears rolling down her cheeks. "You can have the fucking money, I just want to make sure my child is okay. That's all I'm asking."

Now, under normal circumstances, I would have relented and allowed her that respect, but this was not one of those times.

I cocked the hammer back on the gun. "I'm not playing with you. The faster you open that safe, the faster you'll get to your kid. Now, I'm not gon' ask you one more time. Open that fucking safe or I'm blowing your brains out, and then your son's."

"Fuck you! Kill me, then! Kill me, you son of a bitch, because I'm going to get my kid right now!" She ran for the door with her fists balled, swinging them blindly.

I was just about to pop her in the knee when Cavali came through the door holding her son in a full Nelson. The little boy was kicking his legs and struggling to break free.

"Drop him on the bed, boss." I turned to her. "You see, he's straight. Now open that safe or he won't be."

"You're real tough, you know that? You and your guy, both of you are real tough. Just wait until my baby daddy find out who you are. I swear he's going to kill you in cold blood."

She crawled back to the closet and began working on the safe while I knelt beside her. She punched in a series of numbers and hit the pound sign.

The whole key pad lit up red, and it did not open.

I watched her do it again, and it was the same result. "Man hurry up. What's taking you so long?" I was starting to panic because it seemed like she didn't know what she was doing.

She did the same sequence of numbers again, and the same thing happened. "Fuck, I don't know what I'm doing wrong," she said more to herself than me. She took a deep breath and started to rub her temples. "This just has to be happening today. I should have went out of town like I was planning, but no, I had to stay here in fucking

Chicago for my class reunion. Stupid, stupid, stupid." She smacked the palm of her hand against her forehead.

"Look, I don't care about none of that. You better open up this safe or it's about to get real bloody in this room, that's my word." I was thinking about popping her in her knee again. Something just didn't feel right.

"Yeah, well, I guess we're about to die, then, because clearly I don't know the freaking combo. What do you want me to do? I am trying my best!"

This broad had to be bipolar or something, because one minute she was the humble hostage, and the next she was fearless.

"Yo, fuck this. I ain't about to play with her," Cavali said, picking up her son by the neck. He held him in the air and squeezed. The little boy began turning bright red. "Bitch, either you open that safe, or your son is dead. One way or the other, it don't matter to me, but I definitely didn't come out here for nothing." He squeezed tighter and the little boy stopped kicking his legs.

"Okay, okay!" She turned around and popped the safe so fast she broke a nail doing it.

I nodded at Cavali and he dropped the little boy, who did not move. She ran over and picked him up, and I grabbed a pillow off the bed and started loading it up with stacks of money.

I tied the case in a knot and motioned for Cavali to snatch the pair up so we could bind them together. He grabbed the woman by her hair and threw her on the bed on her stomach. Taking a piece of wire, he bound her hands and did the same to the little boy, who was awake and now crying.

We left the bedroom door open on the way out and made our way down the stairs just as somebody was coming into the house from the garage.

Cavali was spotted right away, and before he could up his weapon, there was a loud blast from the kitchen. The bullet slammed into his shoulder and turned him all the way around.

I fell to the ground and shot twice, hitting the masked man in the stomach. He fired another shot that slammed into the television screen, knocking it from the wall and causing it to explode.

The front door opened and three men ran inside and ducked behind the couch. I fired at them and ran toward the garage. Cavali tried to stand up and was hit with a flurry of bullets. His body vibrated in the air before slumping downward.

I ran into the garage and opened the back door to the woman's car, and lucky I did, because she had left the keys on the backseat. I grabbed them and slid into the front as one of the men shot and shattered the driver's side window. Glass splattered all over me and even went inside of my mask. I started the car and backed it out of the garage, shooting in the direction of the kitchen. I ran over the little boy's Bigwheel on the way out and left tire marks all over their lawn, but I made it away.

They must have had a car ducked off somewhere, because one was behind me immediately, firing shots. This was blowing me, because not only had I just lost my li'l homie while we were on a mission, but now I had some fools chasing me through a residential area. It was only a matter of time before the police got involved.

Another shot was fired, causing the back window to shatter. I swerved and skinned a car on the side narrow street and took a hard right at the stop sign. The car behind did the same thing and fired more shots, one wound up hitting the front windshield and made it look like it was about to cave in at any second.

I was moving on pure adrenalin. I kept having the feeling I was about to get shot. I needed to lose whomever it was following me, and I had to do it soon.

I took a strong left down an alley just as it began to rain. In my rearview mirror, the car chasing me did the same. I punched the speed up to 90 miles an hour, smashing into a plastic garbage can that was in the middle of the alley, sending trash flying everywhere. More shot rang out as I came to the end of the alley that turned into a busy street. I turned right and entered the traffic and increased my speeds.

Behind me, I heard the screeching of brakes, and then the sound of cars crashing into each other. I turned around in time to see the car that was chasing me involved in a pretty nasty accident with a bread truck.

I took another right, and circled back around to my truck and disposed of old girl's car.

T.J. & Jelissa

Chapter 12

Ariana

It had been a whole day since I had seen Roman, and I was starting to get worried because he'd left the house pretty pissed off after Jaheim had made a mockery of him. I just hoped he was okay. Not to mention I had a throbbing in my lower region that was screaming his name. I needed him so bad I could barely walk straight.

I heard mumbling outside, so I looked out the front window and saw Jackie standing in front of a man in a BMW-M5, black-on-black with gold Denaro rims. He was well-dressed in a suit and looked as if he had a lot of money. I wondered why he'd be talking to her, so I went outside and got nosey. I walked right down the steps and put my arm on her shoulder, looking at him.

"Excuse me, but who are you?"

"Girl, this is A'Jhani." She gave me a look that said I must have been crazy to not know who he was, and I gave her a look that said I didn't. "You know, A'Jhani. The one that owns all of the strip clubs from here to New York City?" I still didn't know who he was, and that irritated her. She rolled her eyes, and sucked her teeth. "Anyway, he wants me to become one of his dancers and to appear in his magazines and a few hip hop videos." She cheesed her gap-toothed grin, looking at him from the corner of her eye.

He extended his hand. "How are you, love?"

I saw he wore a Rolex watch, and that made me start to take him serious. He smelled good, too, the closer I got to him, so that was a plus. I looked him up and down. "I'm doing quite fine. I'd like to know why you're out here selling my sister all of these dreams. I hope at least 50 percent of what you're saying is true." I batted my eyelashes at him.

He laughed. "One hundred percent of what I am saying is true. Your sister has a body men would pay for to touch, see, and smell. I'm willing to place her under contract and give her a healthy signing bonus." He licked his lips and smiled at Jackie.

She blushed. "Where would you want me to be stationed? I know you got clubs all across the country." She waved a fly away and zoomed in on his eyes. I could tell she was smitten with him.

"To be honest, at first I'd want you to travel with me because I see something in you that screams more than an employee or worker. I want you to be my woman, even if just for a little while. Trust me, it comes with a lot of benefits. You'll be rich in less than a year." He pulled out a cigar and lit it.

"Less than a year? Shid, I wanna be down, too. How can I get down on that same game plan?" I asked, trying to get in where I fit in.

He grabbed me by the shoulder so fast, turned me around, and gripped my butt. He massaged it and even pulled it apart. "I can make a little money off that, but overall you're just another pretty face. This here," he said, reaching for Jackie and gripping her ass, "is prime, baby. This is a million-dollar body, and its fresh." He sucked on to his bottom lip and shook his head.

That definitely crushed my self esteem, because once again I was being rejected by someone. My feelings were hurt. I didn't even know what else to say, so I didn't say anything further at all.

He and Jackie went on talking while I slowly made my way into the house. I went into my room, closed my bedroom door, and cried my eyes out. I wondered why nobody wanted me and why it was such a task for anyone to care about me. I started to feel suicidal, and thought *this is what my mother must have felt like before she took her own life.* I felt like that on most days. I didn't know if I actually had it in me to do something like that, but some days I definitely contemplated it.

Jackie came in the room and slammed the door. "What the fuck is your problem, Ariana? You almost screwed that up for me out there." She walked over to me and stood by my shoulder, looking down on me like I had lost my mind.

"What are you talking about?" I stood up and looked her in the eye. I was not in the mood to back down to her. I felt like I needed some sort of pain to validate what I was feeling, anyway, so maybe I needed a good fight.

"You know what I mean. You brought your high-yellow ass down there and tried to steal away my opportunity. That's not cool. I'm trying to do something that will help my future. I don't want to be stuck in Chicago my whole life." She rolled her eyes and bumped me as she walked past.

I pushed her in the back, causing her to stumble onto her bed.

She bounced up and ran into my face. "Don't be puttin' your fucking hands on me! I'm not your child."

She pushed me and I stumbled backward, then lashed forward, tackling her. We fell to the floor, wrestling. She tried to pin me down, and I was trying to do the same to her. I could not let her get the better of me, although I could tell she was a lot stronger than I.

She wound up getting on top of me with her knee pressed firm between my legs. She held my shoulders down and I could not move.

"Let me up, Jackie, you bitch. Get the fuck off of me."

I tried to pump upward, but she was not moving an inch.

"What are you going to do if I don't? Huh? What can you really do right now, other than stay pinned down in total submission to me?"

She moved her knee more firmly against my kitty. I could feel my sex lips smush together. I turned my hips this way and that, trying to pry apart her grip, but nothing was working. Finally I reached up and ripped her thin blouse. Her brown breasts came tumbling out, both nipples already erect in the cool air. I reached and grabbed ahold of them, pulling them for all they were worth. "Let me up!"

She hollered and held me down even more, her head tilted to the ceiling. She let out a moan and slid her hand under my tennis skirt. I felt her pulling my panties to the side aggressively.

The next thing I knew, her fingers were in me and stabbing me at full speed while I held my legs wide open, sucking on her breasts, switching from one to the next. I bounced all over the floor, not being able to maintain my composure. I flopped around like a fish out of water. The faster her fingers went into me, the crazier I got.

She must have had me on that floor for a whole hour, driving me insane. Afterward, I sat cross-legged on the floor by her bed.

"Jackie, have you ever thought about killing yourself?" I could not even look her in the eyes as I asked this question. I don't even know why I had the nerve to ask her the question in the first place. I guess I was simply feeling so alone, and I just needed to bond with someone.

"What, wait? Ariana, why would you ask me something like that?" She turned off her tablet and sat on the floor beside me, wrapping her arm around my shoulder. "Is there something on your mind you'd like to talk about?"

I lay my head on her shoulder. "Yeah, I been thinking about taking my life a lot lately. I'm just tired of living and tired of being rejected. I feel like the other side is better than this life." I took a deep breath and swallowed.

Jackie pulled on my hair and ran her fingers through it. "What if the next life is way worst than this one? If you found that out to be true, wouldn't you just feel horrible for rushing to get there so much sooner than your time?"

I felt she had a really good point. I didn't know what was going on with me. I guess I just needed somebody to truly love and appreciate me because I had never had that. I needed just one person all to myself, a person who only cared about me and would do anything for me. I mean, I had my mother, but I could tell I was more of an afterthought to her. She was completely consumed with what was taking place with my sister, and I understood that. I just couldn't help the depression that had overtaken me.

"You know what, Jackie? I don't know what the next life holds, but what I do know is this one is taking a toll on me." Tears ran down my face. "Why is it nobody addresses the fact Jaheim is my father? I mean, it's the biggest elephant in the room, yet no one says anything." Tears sailed down my cheeks, and I held on to Jackie tighter.

"Shouldn't you be asking me this question, Ariana?" my mother said, standing in the doorway with Leah behind her.

***

Tiny

I'd been standing outside of the doorway long enough. I did not know Ariana was feeling this way. I had tried my best to not neglect her. I tried to pay her as much attention as I possibly could. To hear her speak in terms of suicide took me back to the days of her mother. She was the exact same age when she took her own life, so that scared me.

Ariana shot up out of Jackie's arms and stood up, rubbing her shoulders as if she were cold. "Mom, how long have you been standing there?" she asked, looking at the ground. I noted their room had a loud odor of sex in the air. I looked them both over slowly and suspiciously.

I stepped further inside and took a seat at the desk where their laptop sat. I took a deep breath because I really didn't know what I wanted to say or do in that moment. I had so much going through my mind. Today was supposed to have been the deadline for Alexis' first payments. We had gotten another message from Jaheim in the middle of last night, and I'd handed the phone right to Roman. I had not seen him, or it, ever since then.

"I've been standing in the hallway long enough to know you haven't felt welcome here, and I haven't been doing the best job of letting you know I love you with all of my heart." I lowered my head and Leah came into the room and rubbed my back.

"Mom, it's not that you haven't been doing your job, because you have." She shook her head. " I don't know, I guess I just feel like, in some sort of way, this is all my fault. I mean, for God's sake, this man is my father, and nobody talks about that."

Jackie came and put her arm around her shoulders. "It's okay, Ariana. You can't be blamed for who your father is. You are an amazing girl, and we all love you. None of us holds that against you. I mean, how could we?" She turned Jackie around and Ariana placed her face into her chest while Jackie rubbed her back.

"I just don't understand why we've never addressed the issue, Mom. Like, why is it everyone walks around and avoids that huge fact? Am I a constant reminder to you of who he is and what you don't have in Alexis right now?" She faced me with tears running down her face. Her nose was starting to run, and she kept swallowing as if she were on the verge of a major breakdown.

"I don't know, baby. I don't know why I have never talked to you about this fact. I guess I felt if we didn't address it, then it would not give it so much power. We know who he is to you, but we also know who you are to us, and that is what's most important."

I fanned my face because their room was a little stuffy. "Leah, get up and turn that thermostat down some. It feels like we're being cooked.

She got up and followed my directives. After she finished, she came right back over and sat at my feet, placing her head on my thigh. She was always under me. No matter where I was in the house, for some reason she was always there, also. I just chalked it up to the fact she loved my daughter so much.

"Ariana, how long have you been thinking about taking your own life? And what steps have you taken to actually go that route?" I needed to know because just listening to her, she sounded exactly like her mother had sounded before she ended it all.

"I've been feeling this way, Mom, for my whole life, but just over the last few months the urges have gotten worse. I think about it all the time, especially when I am rejected by someone or denied love in any fashion." She placed her face into the palms of her hands. "I don't know, Mom. I mean, I get that I'm screwed up, but what do I do?"

I stood and grabbed her from Jackie. Placing my arms around her, I held her as firmly as I could. She wrapped her arms around my waist and placed her face against my own, her tears wetting my cheeks and dripping down to my neck. I held her like that for several seconds, squeezing her tighter and not wanting to let her go.

I started to have flashbacks of when she was just a little premature baby, smaller than the palm of my hand. The doctors had said she wouldn't make it past a week, that she was not strong enough for life outside of the womb. They said we should have been making arrangements for her infant death, and they only gave her a one percent chance of surviving.

Yet here she was, alive and well.

"Baby, I love you, and I know you are strong because you have come from under so much. You are a fighter, and it's not in you to give up." I kissed her forehead. "Do you know that they didn't even give you more than a one percent chance of surviving when you were born?"

"Really, Mom?"

"Yes, those old doctors said you would not make it through the week. They said me and your mom would have to make arrangements to bury you. But you are here, baby, and you're a fighter. You are a champion. Just think about all you have been through and all you have overcome within your 18 years of living. You cannot give up now." I held her tighter. "You see, there is something in you that your mother passed along. It's called severe depression. Your mother had the same illness. That illness tells you that you are mentally and emotionally hurting so bad that life doesn't make sense for you. It tells you things are far worse most times than they really are, and it makes you want to give in and give up on life.

"But what you have to realize is it is all in your mind. Baby, you are a warrior. Besides, would you really want to leave me like that?" My voice began to crack up. "Why would you want to put me through that pain? Can't you see I am already hurting? Do you have any idea what it was like to fight for you every single day in the beginning of your life?" I tried to maintain my composure.

Ariana tightened her hold on me. "Mom, I know you have been through a lot. I know this situation with my sister is breaking you down, and you have told me time and time again how hard it was for you to be by my side in the early days of my life. I know you have always tried to be there for me. I know all of this." She sighed loudly. "I just wish I could change my brain. I wish my mother didn't give me this part of her, because I am having a hard time controlling it."

"But you have to, baby. You absolutely have to, because we need you around here." I took a step back and looked over the rest of the girls in the room. "Isn't that right, girls?"

I looked around the room and everybody had tears in their eyes. We ended this discussion by having a hugging session.

I was on my way out before something else crossed my mind. "Hey, girls, why don't you step out of here for a minute and let me talk to Jackie? It's important." I reached over and grabbed Jackie's hand. She looked up to me as if she were nervous and afraid.

After the girls stepped out of the room, Jackie stood before me, balancing the weight of her body from one foot to the next. "Ms. Johnson, what's the matter? Are you kicking me out of here or something?" She put a finger into her mouth and began biting on the nail.

I shook my head. "No, I would never do anything like that. Why would that even come to your mind?" I asked, giving her a crazy look. Sitting on her bed, I patted the spot next to me.

She sat down and crossed her big thighs. "No, it's just that I know you said you had been in the hallway outside of our room for a while, and I just thought you might've heard something else." At saying this, she blushed and turned her face away from me.

I played the fool. I knew what she was hinting at, but I decided to throw her a momentary bone. "No," I lied. "The reason I wanted to talk to you is because I saw that man out there earlier today, and I know who he is. My question to you is, are you really ready for that kind of a lifestyle?"

She shrugged her shoulders. "I don't really know. I mean, it would be different, and at least I'd be doing something with my life, because right now I am not. I'm 18 years old, and I have absolutely nothing going for myself." She shook her head. "I can't live off of you guys forever. Very soon I'm going to have to find my own way. Life isn't free. Everything comes with a price."

"Okay, I see that you've got that understanding, but how much are you willing to pay?" I looked her over closely. We sat thigh-by-thigh on the bed. I could smell her natural, womanly scent. She smelled as if she were in need of a shower. She wasn't funky, but I could tell it was just time.

She shrugged her shoulders. "I'm willing to pay whatever price I have to in order to get ahead. I don't like being broke, and I desire a certain type of lifestyle. I want to be spoiled. I need to be spoiled. There is no way around it, so whatever I gotta do, I'm going to do it."

I got up, locked the door, and sat back on the bed. "So, you mean to tell me no price is too high for you to pay to become successful?"

She shook her head. "Nope, I'm with whatever will get me there. Nothing that A'Jhani's going to put me through can be worse than what I've already been through in life. I have been hurt so much I am numb to pain. I just don't care anymore. I mean, at least Ariana has the balls to consider suicide. Me, I'm way too weak for that. I know I can't kill myself because if I could, I would have a long time ago."

She got up and stood in front of the mirror. I noted her shorts were so far up her butt it was like she was wearing a thong. I couldn't help but ogle her body, it was that nice.

"Do you know A'Jhani also sells pussy? That most of his girls start out living the good life, but in the end they wind up drowning?" I stood up, preparing to leave the room. "You know he only wants you for your body."

She laughed, reached behind herself and squeezed her booty. Pulling the shorts further up her backside, she spread her legs and bent forward slightly. "So did my father." She smacked herself on the butt. "That's the reason my mother put me in foster care to begin with. My father could not keep his hands off of me, and how could he when I was walking around with all of this ass and my mother barely had any?" She rubbed her hands in a circle all around her globes, even pulled them apart to show the bit of cloth in between. "I know what men see when they look at me, and it's okay. If my dad loved it and couldn't keep his hands off, then why should other men?"

I watched her slide her hand into the front of her shorts and spread her legs as if she were a stripper. I saw the cloth moving under her. I was paying such close attention to her show that I did not know she was eyeing me in the mirror.

"As much as my mother beat me for my father's sins, she also could not keep her hands off of me. She said as much as she hated me, she loved my body and what I did to her." Jackie ran her tongue across her lips. "Ms. Johnson, I see the way you look at me. You remind me of her, and I know you want me just as bad, and I would love if you had me."

Now she leaned completely over the vanity, and I watched from behind as her fingers went in and out of her. She yanked the cloth to the side so I could see it more clearly.

I didn't know what to say. I had to admit she had me spellbound. I found her antics intriguing, and my body responded in kind. I was mentally trapped inside of her show, and I wanted to see what she would do next.

122

Here fingers slid in and out of her box, I could see that as clear as day. She stopped and smashed her lips together, spread them, and pushed her fingers back into her cave, moaning deep within her throat.

"It's okay, Ms. Johnson. You can watch me. I love for people to just look at me. I love to be desired and everything that comes along with it." She sped up the pace, growling deep within her throat.

I watched her cheeks jiggle as she manipulated herself. "Stop that, little girl," I whispered. "What's the matter with you?" My breathing got heavy and my heart was beating so fast I thought I would pass out if it didn't slow down some. I couldn't believe how my body was reacting at a time like that. I had juices running all down my legs, and my knees were starting to buckle. I took a step forward toward her, even though my brain screamed for me to stop. "Jackie, you need to stop that. I'm serious," I said so low I barely heard myself saying it.

She leaned all the way over and spread her legs, pulling her shorts to the side even more. "Touch my pussy, Ms. Johnson. Come on, please touch my little pussy. I know you know what you're doing because you're a vet, and you've been locked down for a while, just like my father's girlfriend was, and she was a beast when it came to freaking me. So touch me, please. I so desperately need you to. "She waved her ass from side to side, enticing me.

"Please don't do that, Jackie. Not right now. I'm going through so much mentally that I can't be responsible for what I'm going to do to you." By that time my juices were leaking out of me so bad I had to put a hand between my own legs just to feel my heat. My lips were engorged, and my panties were soaking wet. I didn't know what was getting into me. Maybe it was the fact I needed a distraction. I needed something to take my mind off what was taking place with my child. I know that sounded crazy, but I had been thinking about it every second of every day, so much so I was starting to become physically sick. I needed some sort of release. I needed to open up another channel of myself.

Jackie turned around, walked up to me, and kissed me right on the lips, sucking passionately. She grabbed my booty and squeezed it as if she were a hungry dude.

That drove me crazy. I moaned into her mouth. I felt her sliding her hand down the front of my biker shorts and spread my legs. Her fingers separated my sex lips and went inside of me. She picked up my right leg and dove her fingers into me again and again while I balanced myself on one foot, moaning like I had lost my mind.

"Tell me you love it, Ms. Johnson. Tell me you love how I make you feel and that you been lusting over me ever since you first saw me."

She sped up her assault on my pussy. I couldn't believe how she was treating me, but one thing for sure was I needed it. I needed to take my mind off things for a while.

I don't know how it happened, or even when it happened. All I remember was her stopping, sliding her hand up the bed, and the next thing I knew she had me bent over on all fours, screwing me from the back with a strap-on. She threw a pillow on the floor and I buried my face into it, screaming at the top of my lungs while she screwed me so good, I damn near wanted to go and cook her a meal afterward.

Chapter 13

Roman

Last night was most definitely crazy. I had somehow managed to escape the niggas that were chasing me. I don't know if fate stepped in, or maybe it was God Himself. Either way, I was able to make a clean getaway. I had lost Cavali along the way, but losing a homey was a part of the territory. I'd make sure his kids were straight for as long as I was alive. I'd even reach for his baby mother. We both entered into that mission last night knowing there was a chance one or both of us could have been killed. It was a risk we were both willing to take. It just sucked that he wound up striking out.

There was only 75 thousand in the safe, along with four bricks of heroin. That cash brought my total to 250 thousand . Later on that night I had my li'l ones run in that spot up the street where they recovered another 200 bands. So, all in all, I had $450,000. I was fifty away from the total I needed to make it happen for Alexis.

The phone vibrated at five in the morning on Monday. Jaheim's ugly face appeared.

"Nigga, you got my money?" he asked with a bottle of champagne in his hand. This time his background was different. It no longer looked like he was in some sort of dungeon. It looked as if he were in a house of some sort, because in the background I could see a stove and cabinets. In fact, he was sitting at a table actually having breakfast. This fool had some nerve.

I was already in my truck headed to the spot he had given me last night when he'd called Ariana's phone. "Yeah, I got your money, homie. What's good with my li'l cousin, though?" I needed to see her. I needed to make sure she was okay and in the best of health.

He stuffed his mouth with a fork full of food, chewed it for a little while, then grabbed the bottle of champagne to wash it down. He took another bite and repeated the same process. "You know what kills me about you, nigga? You still think you're in charge of everything. You think just because you got that punk-ass money, that gives you the right to demand shit. Haven't you learned that pissing me off only makes things worse off for her?" He turned the bottle of pink champagne up and drank it as if he was trying to finish the whole bottle.

I was getting tired of his charade. I was sick of playing by his rules already, and it was so hard for me to not let him know that. I was praying there would be an opening down the line for me to catch him and murder him in cold blood. That was on my mind every second of every day. "You know what, Jaheim? I know you're in charge, homie. I just wanted to see my li'l cousin, that's all. I stay worried about her at all times. I mean, I should at least have that right."

He laughed. "Oh, you worried about her, huh? Well, ain't that just sweet of you?" He stuffed his mouth again with his fork of food, smacking so loud it was like ten people were around him, eating with their mouths wide open. He washed it down with the champagne. "You just worry about having my funds in order, and I'll worry about Alexis' wellbeing, because right now she belongs to me. I'll see you in a minute. "He hung up and the feed went blank.

So, he was going to be there, also. That was news to me. I didn't think he'd have enough balls to meet me in person, but maybe I had him pegged all wrong. My only problem was I didn't know how I was going to handle meeting with this dude and not losing my temper. Just seeing his face over the phone made my blood run hot, so I could only imagine what would take place seeing him in person.

He wanted to meet by the old train station behind the bridge on 57th Avenue. It was an old railway yard that was now deserted. Many of the hustlers that I knew went here to do their business. I don't know why they chose that spot, but it was widely popular. I had done some dirt there a few times over the years. I personally liked the spot because it was in the open. There was nowhere to hide, and there was only one entrance and one exit, so it lessened the chances of there being any foul play. I didn't know what Jaheim had on his mind, but to me, this rail yard was my turf, I knew how to navigate around the entire area. I had a couple of my shooters in place just in case things did take a turn for the worse. I wasn't expecting no bloodshed, but I definitely wasn't about to be caught off guard if there just so happened to be some. I was already prepared to go out with guns blazing. I would peep the situation closely, and if I felt like he was on something other than what he was supposed to be on, I was signaling for my shooters to let loose. The only thing that would change my perspective is if he showed up with my li'l cousin.

That's exactly what happened about twenty minutes later. Jaheim rolled up in a fire-red Chevy Caprice classic with a brown van following close behind him. He saw me standing on the side of my truck with the bookbag full of money and pulled up beside me, rolling down his window. "Nigga, tell them fools to go home or I'm about to give the word to have your li'l cousin bodied!" He said this through clenched teeth. "You forget I'm from the land, and it ain't a spot in this city I don't know about and how to cover. Your men don't even know how to be covert. I spotted they ass a mile away. Now, tell them to bounce or shit about to get real serious, real fast," he hissed, putting his phone to his ear.

Something in me wanted to put the gun to his head and pull the trigger. I wanted to knock his noodle straight into his lap and laugh my head off. I hated this fool, and I couldn't wait to get my chance to torture his ass. I meant that.

"Alright, homie. You got me, but my boys were just here for security, just making sure everything stay on the up-and-up." I gave the signal that told them to ride out. From a distance I could see it returned, and then I watched as their whips filed out and disappeared. "Alright, now they gone. Let's get down to business."

He gave me a look of disgust. "Nigga, once again you making it seem like you're calling the shots. We'll get shit on the road when I'm ready to." He pulled out a mirror, sat it on his lap, and dumped some white powder onto it from a vial. I watched him lower his head and snort the substance up one of his nostrils, and then the other. He coughed and smiled. "That's the shit I'm talking about, right there."

He stuck his hand out of his window and twirled it in a circle. The van's door slid open, and out came two masked men. They reached back inside the van, and I saw Alexis appear with duct tape around her mouth. She had on the same clothes she'd been wearing the last time I saw her, before she was abducted. She looked five pounds lighter. I almost ran to her, but I had to keep my composure.

128

The two men that had her pulled out their assault rifles and held them on each side of her temples.

"Come on, Jaheim, is all that necessary? She's just a kid."

I saw the tears rolling down her cheeks and knew she would be forever scarred. I didn't understand how a man could take a young female through so much. He had to have an intense hatred for Tiny to do all of this.

Jaheim got out of the car, and I noted his female driver got out as well and held a gun pointed directly at me. She had a mask on that only covered half of her face, but I could see her eyes screamed death. She looked like she was itching to kill me. I felt a shiver go down my spine and had a vision of them killing both me and Alexis and taking the money. I mean, what was there to stop them?

"Yeah, it's all relative, player. You see, this is how I get down. I like to treat muthafuckas how they should be treated. I do unto others as they do unto me. That's just how that shit gotta go." He looked over at Alexis and shook his head. "This li'l bitch been crying every since she been with me. I don't think I'm that bad of a host." He shrugged his shoulders. "I don't know. Is that my money in that bag?" He reached and grabbed it off of my shoulders roughly.

The sun had come out and was beaming so hard I started sweating immediately. I felt sweat rolling all down my back. Birds were flying all above us and making loud screeching noises as if they were vultures preparing for somebody to be killed.

"Yeah, that's your money, all 300 gees of it, just like we agreed." I felt the humidity starting to thicken the air. I watched him closely and noted his driver did not take her eyes off me for one second. She looked at me as if she hated my very presence.

He took the bookbag and opened it, looked inside, and smiled. "Yo, what the fuck you out here doing that you can come up wit' this type of money this fast?" He looked at me from the corner of his eye. "I ain't never heard about you, and your name ain't ringing in these streets, so what's really good?"

He stepped to me and ripped my shirt down the middle, exposing my bulletproof vest. "A vest?" he laughed. "This fuck-nigga got the nerve to be wearing a vest like he expecting us to shoot at his chest if we gon' shoot." He laughed again, this time way louder than before. "Bitch nigga, don't you know we aim at that head? Our goal is to knock that peanut off of your shoulders. Fuck that vest." He smacked it with his hand. "Take that shit off. I gotta make sure you ain't wearing no wire. Ain't no way in hell you came up with this money on your own."

He began ripping the vest off of me, stripping me like I was a female being raped. I felt so emasculated. "Yo, nigga, chill. I got it." I took the vest off and threw it on the ground. "I ain't wearing no fucking wire. This ain't pig business; this is street business. Besides, you know damn well they ain't about to put up no 300 gees for a black girl. That shit'd never happen."

He turned me around and began searching me, taking my gun off my hip and placing it onto his. He patted me down from head to toe, then flipped me back around and stepped into my face. "You know what, playboy? You got a lot of nerves. You actually had the audacity to bring a gun to this meeting." He laughed and turned around to look at his henchmen. "I guess he really think he's their hero or something."

He leaned all the way to the right and backhanded me with his left, then pulled me up and spit in my face. "If you ever pull some shit like that again, I'll kill you right where you stand. That's my word." He breathed into my face as if he were out of breath. "I don't like you. I don't like your punk-ass cousin, and I don't like that bitch behind me because she came out of the womb of your punk-ass cousin. I can't even bring myself to fuck her because I hate your bloodline so much, so all this is about for me is my money!" He grabbed me by the neck and squeezed with his right hand. "If it wasn't about the money, I'd kill you dead right where you stand." He pushed me backward by my neck and walked over to Alexis. "You see your cousin over there? This nigga done gave me $300,000 for your ass! Can you believe that shit? Now, you gotta know you ain't worth one penny of that money." He ripped the tape off of her mouth. "Say something, bitch. Go ahead, thank that nigga." He pointed to me.

"Thank you, Roman. Thank you so much, cousin, and I love you with all that I am," she said, sounding as if she were out of breath. I noted her shaking, and that worried me. She looked like she had not eaten in a long time. I grew concerned for her health.

"You don't worry about that. All you worry about is being strong," I said, wiping the blood and spit from my face. I felt mad as I had ever been. I felt ready to explode, and I was having a hard time controlling myself. I knew I was outnumbered and out-gunned. In fact, I didn't even have a gun anymore because that fool took it. It was killing me to see my people stranded like that, held at gunpoint and being treated all rough. No man, no real man, could ever sit back and watch a woman in his family be treated any kind of way and not do nothing about it. That was the worst feeling in the world to me. "Alexis, I just got a little more paper to get, and then you'll be home, li'l momma. Trust me, I'm on it." I nodded my head to give her some comfort.

Above our heads, a bunch of white birds flew around in circles and occasionally dropped their feces. The sun was picking up steam, and I was feeling like something was about to happen for the worse. I couldn't quite put my finger on it, but I did not feel right.

Jaheim fixed the tape onto Alexis' mouth and grabbed her by her hair. She yelped out in pain, and I had to stop myself from running over to her. I started in her direction, and Jaheim upped a knife and put it to her throat.

"Bring yo' ass over here and I'm gon' cut her throat out. I'm not playing, either." He started to slowly cut her enough so she bled. "Oh, look at this bitch bleed"

"Alright, yo. Chill, man. Yo, I ain't coming over there, just calm down, homie." I held my hands out in front of me in a calming gesture. I did not want to inflame the situation any more. He seemed as if he was already dead-set on hurting her as much as possible, so I couldn't entice him or it wouldn't fair well for either one of us.

"You know what? I can tell you really do love her. I can tell you really do care about this li'l bitch. Now, me personally, I don't know why. Unless, of course, you was hitting this pussy. Wait a minute, that's what this is all about, ain't it? That's why you doing whatever it takes to get this li'l hooker back? It's because you was fucking her li'l young ass, wasn't you?" He smacked himself on the forehead and turned his face toward the sky, laughing at

the top of his lungs from deep within his belly. "Ol'
Roman ain't no savior. Roman just trying to keep him a
fresh slice of young pussy." He smiled, "I ain't mad at
you, dawg. Shid, live and let live. Fuck it." He pointed
toward his car. "You see that fine bitch right there that got
her gun pointed toward you? That's my blood, and I been
wearing that out since the beginning. That's why she's
crazy, just like me. Ain't that right, Brandy?" He said this
looking directly at his driver. In response, she cocked
back her gun and pointed it at me again. "You know, it's
crazy what that forbidden sex can do. It be having
muthafuckas doing the unthinkable."

Not only was I getting so hot I was in a pool of my
own sweat, but on top of that a nasty-ass bird had the
nerve to shit right on my shoulder. I mean, it got me good,
too. It felt like somebody had hit me with a hot snowball.
I felt just like it was: just like shit.

Jaheim started laughing. "Damn, it seem like even the
birds don't like yo' ass." He looked into the sky. "Fuck,
y'all wanna work for me, too? Y'all wanna fuck this
nigga and his family over, too? I promise you, it's the
greatest!" He hollered up at them. "Seeing as you love
this li'l bitch so much, I'm upping the ransom and
shortening the time. I need a whole 500 thousand by
Sunday morning at the crack of dawn. If Sunday comes
and you ain't got all of my money, you'll find her right
here in this spot, cut into a hundred pieces. Wait, fuck
that, that's too many. She'll be in, like, six though.
Anyway, let's not make that happen. I don't feel like
butchering this bitch. I mean, to do that I gotta get all
dirty and shit, then it's already hot outside. I gotta have
the air conditioner all the way up. Then she got a li'l meat

on her, so it'll take more time, and I'm just really not looking forward to doing all of that, so don't make me." I almost lost my mind. "500 more? Where the fuck am I supposed to get that kind of money from?" I wanted to run at that fool. I wanted to just make him kill me, because there was no way I would be able to come up with another 500 stacks in a week. That shit just was not possible.

"Wherever you got it from before, you gon' have to get it again. That shit really ain't my problem. I couldn't care less. You just make sure you have my shit when I hit you up on Sunday, because if not, I'm bodying shorty's ass, and I'm gon' have chunks of her right here in this spot where I'm standing." He made an X sign with his feet in the dirt. "X marks the spot, muthafucka!"

"Jaheim, yo, that wasn't the deal, man. The deal was for me to bring you 300 gees and then hit you with the other 200 later this week." This stud was really blowing me. Something just told me he had his mind set on killing my li'l cousin anyway, no matter how much money we gave him. "Yo, who's to say after you get this money you ain't gon' pull the same shit again?" I asked, feeling the bird shit drip off my shoulder.

Jaheim shook his head. "Nall, I ain't on that next time. You tell Zivial that once y'all come up with that full amount, she'll get her daughter, and she'll be alive and well." He whipped his fingers through the air. "Let's go!"

His men snatched Alexis up and threw her back into the van where the side door was rolled shut. He walked past me and smacked me on the back. "Guess I'll be seeing you soon, my nigga!" He walked off laughing, got in the passenger seat to the red whip, and they all stormed off.

Chapter 14

Ariana

"I'm telling you, girl, all we have to do is have a sit-down with him. Chris' father is super plugged. I'm sure he can help with our situation, especially if all they're talking about is money," Rosie said, biting into her gyro. She had so much meat on there she could barely get her mouth around it to take a bite. She had to hold it with both hands, and even then she spilled a nice bit of it back over her plate.

We were at Aiden's House of Gyros, and I was so hungry I could have eaten a horse. I had a gyro sitting on my plate just as big as hers, and I was about to do my best to tear that sucker up. I started mine of by simply taking some of the big chunks of meat and eating them one-by-one. I knew I could not pick that big boy up without spilling it everywhere.

"How sure are you Chris will be willing to let us talk to his pops? Besides, aren't there some type of major war going on?"

Rosie had her head leaned to the side, trying to stuff as much of the gyro into her mouth so she could bite down on it. When she did, she moaned and shook her head like she could not believe how good it tasted. She put the straw to her pop inside of her lips and sucked up some of the sugary drink.

"I swear every time I come in here their food gets better and better. This shit so good it's making my nipples hard, and I ain't playing, either." She pulled her shirt taut to her chest to show me her nipples protruding. "You see that shit? That means if I could fuck this gyro, I would, and with no hesitation." She took another bite and held her finger up to indicate she needed a minute.

Aiden's was a hole-in-the-wall joint most of the high school students went to from around the corner. It was run by the same two men that had a clothing store that always got the latest gear from the hip hop world of fashion. They were well respected and the hood didn't allow nothing bad to happen to their establishments. I liked the joint because not only was the quality of their food good, but they gave you a lot of it for your money. That was always a plus, especially when you were hungry and didn't have much cash.

"Girl, you can eat that food and talk at the same time." I rolled my eyes and squirted some Tabasco sauce onto my chili cheese fries.

She nodded with her cheeks so big it looked like her head was about to pop off. She took another drink from her pop and burped. "Whew, excuse me," she said, covering her mouth way too late. She took another sip of her pop. "Okay, I know Chris would be willing to get his father involved because the dude that's with your sister and my best friend is also his ace. Them niggas use to bathe in the same tub as kids. They grew up together in the projects. His father, Prince's father and his mom, all of them are connected." She put a fry into her mouth. "Now that Prince has been missing for a little while, they are ready to do whatever it takes to find out where he is. That means getting Chris' father involved because Prince is the name of the boy that went off with your sister and never returned, and he is King's son. King and Chris are best friends, and so are their children. Li'l Chris be having all of them whips and shit because his father is filthy rich. Back in the day, they took over the whole city of Chicago by forcing people to shoot up their heroin. Once they were hooked, they put a whole system in place that left people solely dependent on them. They added some type of special chemical to the dope that caused it to make you feel like you were taking it for the first time every single time. They called it The Virgin." She bit off of her sandwich again.

There weren't many people inside of the place, and it was probably because we were so early, we were literally eating gyros for breakfast. I didn't have a problem with that because I wasn't a huge fan of breakfast food anyway. To me, gyros should have been eaten 24 hours a day. I took another bite and closed my eyes, loving the taste of it as I chewed.

"Li'l Chris feels like it's his fault Prince got snatched up because he was supposed to have went with him, but he wound up handling some other business in Cleveland. He really didn't tell me what it was, but he said it was important. His main thing was hoping he could get Prince back before too much shit started to pop off. Prince's father is already looking at him like it's his fault because he didn't tail him wherever he was supposed to go that day." She shook her head.

I shrugged my shoulders. "I don't know, I think if anybody knew where they were headed that day, it would make things a lot more easy. I can't believe Li'l Chris doesn't know where his right hand man was on his way to. I mean, how tight can they really be if he didn't know that?" I said, letting out a burp of my own.

"I don't know, but here he comes right, now."

We turned to look over our shoulders as a purple and black Bentley GT pulled to the curb, and the Lamborghini door to the driver's side opened up. "Damn, that nigga be getting me wet just off the cars he be driving."

He came into the restaurant and went right to the counter, ordering his food, I assumed. Rosie couldn't even let him finish doing that before she was all over him. They tongued each other down so long that by the time they were done, his food was ready. They walked over to the table with his arm around her. They slid into the booth across from me, first Rosie, then him.

"Yo, this that redbone you was with earlier today when I saw you on the avenue?" He looked across the table at me and smiled.

"Yeah, this her. And don't start jocking her and shit." Rosie rolled her eyes. "You better explain to us what the fuck is going on and what's about to take place, because we're both crazy confused right now. Like, how in the hell did you not know where Prince and my sister where headed?" She turned toward him and ate another fry.

He took a butter knife and cut his Cheeseburger diagonally. "Who said I didn't know where they were supposed to have went? Because I sure did." He took three napkins, put them together, and placed them in his lap. "They were supposed to be conducting some business out in Detroit with some of the fam from the six, but bro an' them said they ain't heard from them, nor did they see them that day, which can only mean they never made it that far. They could be anywhere from here to Detroit. All I know is my pops and King done put up a million dollar reward for Prince's return. They said they willing to get him back by any means. The worst thing you can do is put up that kind of money in the hood. I guarantee you they gon' be popping up real soon, that's the realest. If not, we about to start wrecking whole families in and out of

Chicago. My old man, them ain't playing." He picked up his burger and bit off of it.

Rosie sat frozen. "Damn, they talking about a million dollars cash for him?" She shook her head. "What about Alexis? Why they ain't put shit up for her?" She looked like she was a little angry. She pushed her half-eaten sandwich away from her and sat back with her arms crossed around her body.

That must have been her typical mannerisms because Li'l Chris didn't pay her no mind at all. "You already know that wherever she is, he is. So, if they wind up getting him back, they'll get her as well. "

"How do you know that, though? Who's to say since there is no reward for her they won't simply turn him over and kill her?" I started to worry about my sister. Even though I didn't really know her like that, I still loved her, and I wanted her home.

"I'm pretty sure that's not how it's going to happen, but that's another reason why I want us to sit down with my old man. That way we can get a better understanding as to what's what and how we're going to do things. Besides, he wants to meet your mother, especially if the dude that has y'all sister and her have history. She should be able to tell us a little bit about him and how he thinks. We need to know how to go at this dude and who all he got rolling with him." He turned to me. "Do you know who this nigga is?"

I shook my head. "Nope, I never met him before. But my mother does, and she'll definitely be open to helping your father track him down." I thought about my mother getting this news and being extremely happy. The assistance would help her ease some of her anxieties. The last time I saw her, she looked like a nervous wreck, like at any moment she was going to lose her mind.

Li'l Chris nodded, "Then that's what we're going to do. We gon' roll out and scoop her up. Then we gon' meet up with my old man at his palace out in Harrisburg. I'm gon' call him ahead of time to get the okay, but I know it's good, though." He ate some more of his burger while Rosie looked him over as if she wanted to eat him.

Something in my soul just did not feel right. I felt like I was missing something, but I didn't know what it was. Suddenly, I felt sick to the stomach, and as if I was ready to throw up. I pushed myself away from the table and ran to the bathroom only to find it was occupied. I beat on the door to the women's room and some lady screamed she was in there. My only option was to go into the Men's, which I did. I made it only a part of the way inside before I was throwing up everywhere. I mean, I could not stop myself. I was throwing up so much that my stomach was lurching inward. I didn't know what was wrong with me.

***

Tiny

I sat in the back seat next to Ariana, thinking about what Jackie and I did the night before. I was starting to feel guilty, and I noted her and I couldn't even look each other in the eyes anymore. It was a much-needed fix, yet one I was starting to regret. I felt Ariana lay her head on my shoulder, and that made me think about Alexis. I wondered how my baby was doing and if she had eaten anything at all. The last time I saw her on the phone, she looked noticeably skinnier.

"Morn, how are you doing?" Ariana asked.

She kissed me on the shoulder and rubbed my back. I could tell something was bothering her. I just couldn't quite put my finger on it. "I'm ready to get your sister back, baby, and I am hoping whomever this man is will be able to help us do exactly that. I miss her so much." I exhaled.

"I know. We all do, Mom. Trust me, she'll be home soon, and then all of this will be behind us." She kissed me on the cheek and lay her head back onto my shoulder.

"Yo, Ms. Johnson, my Pops one hunnit. All you gotta do is let him know exactly what you know and he gon' make sure we get your daughter and my brother back. Money talks the same all over the world, so whoever got them can't go nowhere without hearing our conversation, you feel me?"

"Yeah, Ms. Johnson, it's all good. I've met his dad a few times, and he seems pretty down to earth. I know they want the same thing you do. We all do, so let's work as a team so we can get my best friend back. I've been thinking about her

every single day, and I can't wait to be reunited with her again. I just pray she is alive and well." She said this as if it was an afterthought. She turned back around in her seat and lay her head onto Li'l Chris's shoulder.

Hearing her last comment made shivers run up and down my spine. I got the chills like I had never had them before. I didn't want to imagine my daughter not being alive and well. I prayed silently to the Lord above that she was okay. I needed her so bad. I hated the fact she had to pay for my sins against Jaheim, although I couldn't quite put my finger on what I had really done to him to make him hate me so much. If anything, I had actually saved his daughter's life. I didn't understand why he did not see things the way they really were, but I guess that's what happens when you look through the yes of a lunatic.

Thirty minutes later, we were sitting at a round table inside a den. The lights were dimmed and I could smell lavender. The space was cramped, and the air was quite thick from humidity.

Ariana sat to my left and Rosie to my right. Li'l Chris sat on the other side of Rosie to her right, and to Ariana's left was an empty chair. I was guessing that was where Chris would sit.

I kept getting these chills that ran done my spine, and for some reason I was starting to feel uneasy. I wished Roman would have not been so secretive with what he had going on in regards to my daughter. I mean, he didn't give me any intel at all. I wondered if he was making any headway.

I was off deep inside my head when we heard movement in the hallway behind us.

Chris jumped up. "Yo, that must be my dad and King right there." He opened the door and we waited to see who came across the threshold. In the background was the sound of light jazz music. It was nice and mellow. I was still having a hard time relaxing. Chris looked as if he couldn't wait for his father to step into the room. As soon as he got partway into the door, the younger Chris hugged his old man.

I smiled and looked off. I started to miss Alexis and tried to remember what it felt like to hug her the last time I did. I remember noting she was a little bit taller than me, and she felt incredibly soft. I melted into my baby, and for that moment I was not in prison. I was somewhere far away from it all with her. We were both together in our safe haven. I felt my eyes starting to water. I fanned them and looked back to the front of the room where Chris was finishing his hug with his father.

He turned toward us. "Dad, this Rosie, Ariana, and Ms. Johnson. She's the lady I was telling you about whose daughter was with Prince when he disappeared."

The older Chris nodded in understanding and looked me over, squinting his eyes. "Shorty, you look real familiar to me, like I have seen you somewhere before. Do you know me?" he asked, lowering the slits of his eyes.

It didn't take me no time at all to recognize him. As soon as I heard his voice, it all came back to me. The older Chris was the one that kidnapped me along with Alexis' father back in the day. He'd beat Avery senseless all because Avery, Alexis' father, had vouched for a man to enter into their organization, and he turned out to be a thief and a rat. Because of this, Chris took his anger out on my baby's dad with violence and told me if I ever wanted to see him again, I would have to come up with $70,000. He was the same man I was supposed to meet up with the day I got arrested. So, I didn't know what my answer should be. I didn't know if I should tell him the truth and risk what he might do, or if I should just tell him a lie and pray he didn't recognize me.

I decided to go with the truth. He didn't look like he was one for playing games. "I'm Avery's baby's mother." I lowered my head. "Back in the day, Avery brought some dude into y'all's fold that turned out to be a thief. You took what the other guy did out on him, and you told me if I ever wanted to see him again, I would have to pay you 70 stacks. I had all of the money ready to go, but somebody tried to rob me, and they got killed. Long story

short, I never got a chance to get you your money because
I was taken to prison. I believe you called me by the name
of Tiny back then." I said the last part so low it was
basically a whisper.

He squinted his eyes and rubbed his chin. "Yo, that
was you?" He looked down on me in disbelief.

"That was who?" another man said, coming into the
room with a low cut and deep waves on his head. He was
dressed in a well-tailored Armani suit. He was so
handsome that, for a moment, I forgot I was in danger.

"King, you remember that fuck-nigga Avery the
young radicals stomped into the concrete so bad he
wound of paralyzed from the waist down for the duration
of his life?" He tapped him on the shoulder.

King nodded. "Yeah, I remember, and I think he got
what he deserved. You should never cosign for a nigga
you don't know because when you do, you both lie down
in the same bed, no matter what. I feel like what happened
to him wasn't all that bad.." King adjusted his cufflink on
his right wrist. "So, anyway, what does that have to do
with her?"

"Yo, that's the broad he was with that was swearing
up and down she was gon' get our chips back that was
stolen. She say before she could make that happen, she
got knocked and been down ever since." He turned back
to me and scowled. "Shit starting to look real fishy around
this muthafucka."

King walked over to me and placed his hand on my
shoulder. He smelled like Armani cologne. He smelled
like money. His touch was light, yet firm. "Little lady, do
you have anything against me or my brother right here?"
He pointed with his head to Chris.

I shook my head so fast and hard I brought on a migraine. "No, sir. I had forgotten all about this entire ordeal until I heard his voice. It was only then it took me back to those days. I tried my best to get the money to him on time, it's just this girl tried to rob me, and I wasn't going. I didn't kill her, either, but she did die on my watch, so. But to answer your question, no I do not. All I want is my daughter back, and I am willing to do anything to make that happen."

King knelt down in front of me, and took my hands into his. "How old is your daughter?"

"She's 17 years old. She's just a child." I started to break down.

"Are you sure she was with my son when he went missing? Please keep in mind that every detail is important."

"As far as I know. At least, that's what everyone is telling me. This girl right here knows for sure because they were all together that day before they split up," I said, pointing at Rosie.

Rosie wrapped her arms around Li'l Chris and looked as if she were about to panic. "Please don't kill me, Mr. King. I don't know where they are. Please don't chop my body up. I swear I'll help you in any way I can." She had tears rolling down her cheeks.

"Yo, chill, baby. My uncle ain't even like that. I have never seen him hurt a female before." Li'l Chris said, holding on to her tighter. "Just tell him what you know."

Rosie nodded, refusing to let Li'l Chris's arm go. "Okay. That day Alexis had hit my phone and told me she and Prince were going out of town to make a couple moves. When I asked her where they were going, she said he had not told her, so I told her when she found out to call me and let me know. Sometime later on that night she told me they were in Detroit. That was the last call I got from her, so I don't know what happened after then."

"Are you sure that's all you know?" Chris asked, pulling her and her chair from under the table.

She really looked devastated now. She looked as if she were terrified for her life. "Yes, that is all I know."

"Nephew, I thought you said this man that has my son was her baby father? Why have you brought them here if they are of no use to us?" He looked pissed.

"No, she knows him from way back when. She even knows his name."

"You know his name?" He looked optimistic. There seemed to be a light of hope in his eyes. "What is his name, and where is he from?"

"Jaheim. At least, that's what I know him by. We used to stay in the Stateway Projects and the Robert Taylor homes back in the day. I used to sell pussy for him."

"Jaheim, huh? How do this muthafucka look?" Chris asked, almost growling.

"He's dark skinned, about six feet tall, muscular, with a low haircut. Back in the day he had a heroin and cocaine habit. I don't know what he has now, but clearly there is something wrong with his head."

"Something gotta be wrong with this nigga to me messing with our family," Chris said, clenching his jaw.

"What has he asked of you since he's had your daughter?" King asked, now standing up and dusting off his pants.

"$500,000."

King nodded. "I can deal with this shit if it's just about the money, because we got enough of that. But if it's something personal, then that's another matter altogether."

I was so scared I didn't know what to do. "Is there anything I can do to help you help us?"

King paced back and forth with his eyelids low. He seemed to be in deep thought. "Have you been in contact with this man recently?"

I nodded.

"When, and did you see my son anywhere in the background?"

"He gets in touch with us through Ariana's phone. The last time he did, he was asking about $300,000 that we were supposed to deliver to him yesterday. He was very adamant about killing my daughter if he didn't receive it."

"And this 300 thousand, did you wind up giving it to him?" King asked, stopping in front of me and looking me over closely.

"You see, that's what I don't know." I took a deep breath. "I don't know because my cousin took the phone and said he would handle everything. My only hope is that he was able to come up with the money."

"Who the fuck is your cousin, and why ain't he here right now?" Chris asked, giving me a look that said he was growing irritated.

"My cousin's name is Roman, and the reason he isn't here is because he's out trying to get Alexis back. We didn't tell him we were meeting with you guys." I was starting to tremble.

"Well, I'm gon' need for you to call homie right now and make it happen. I wanna meet with him face-to-face, and I need to do that right away. That name, Roman, sound familiar, too. Where is he from?" Chris asked.

"We're both from the same projects."

Just then, Li'l Chris' phone vibrated. He looked down at it and frowned. "Yo, who could this be trying to Facetime with me?" He started to open up the feed. Once he did, he scooted back so far in his chair he bumped into his father. "Pops, here is Prince, right here."

He handed the phone to King. King made Li'l Chris go run to get a laptop. Once he did, he hooked the feed up to the computer for us all to see.

On the screen we could see Prince tied to a concrete wall by handcuffs and chains. On each side of him were masked goons pointing assault rifles, one to each of his temples. They had on all white, including their ski masks. Another masked goon came into the camera. "King, we have your son, and we need $5,000,000 or this fuck-nigga is dead. We need it in cash, and we need it by tomorrow night at ten o'clock or you will find him just like you found your sister a long time ago. Have the bags of money dropped off at the old railway yard at ten tomorrow night on the dot. There will be a car there with a man wearing a red mask. Give him the bags of money and let him drive away. Do not try any funny business or any tactics. Once he's out of the floods, we'll send you a text where you will find your son alive and in the trunk of a car. You got that?"

King curled his upper lip. "I guess so, homie. Let me ask you a question, though: is $5,000,000 really worth it?"

In response to his question, the screen went black.

"Yo, it's one thing to be fucking with somebody else's kid and trying to squeeze them, but this is our family. And when a muthafucka do something to our family, everybody they know gotta suffer to the millionth degree.

It's been a while since I had a little fun, but I'm about to change all of that. Chris, I guess we're back out here!"

T.J. & Jelissa

Chapter 15

Roman

Where the fuck was I going to get $500,000 from by Monday? I was going over the whole thing in my mind, and it was starting to feel like I was fighting a losing battle. There was no way I was going to be able to fulfill this mission by the deadline.

I got out of my whip, slammed the door, and walked right into Emily's house. I didn't even stop to ring the doorbell. Her maid was in the living room, vacuuming the rug. I walked right past her and stepped on the rug she was vacuuming, straight onto the terrace after opening the glass doors that led out there.

Emily was lounging in the pool, floating on a inner tube with sunglasses on and a big summer hat that was basically a rich girl's sombrero. She had an umbrella drink in her hand and looked like she was relaxing. I walked up to the pool, grabbed the beach ball, and threw it over, trying to hit her. It bounced off the water, and skipped over her body. She sat up and looked over in my direction. I gave her a come-here motion with my forefinger.

She dived into the 25-meter pool and came up right in front of me, wringing her hair out. "Hcy, baby, How have you been?"

"How have I been?" I almost slapped her ass. "I been waitin' for you to get into contact with me about this money. You said you'd have an answer for me by yesterday. What is your answer?"

She put a finger up to her lips. "Calm down. Let's go to my room." She got out of her pool and led the way.

Back in the distance, I could see she had a few friends over and they were using her tennis courts. They were about to make their way over to where we were, but she waved them off. They stopped and turned around with the sun beaming onto their backs. They looked to be two of the same college female buddies I'd seen over at her place before, both skinny blondes with fathers that were well-connected in the political world.

We got to her room and she crashed into me and kissed all over my lips, squeezing my penis through my pants. "Baby, just let me suck you, please."

I smacked her hand away, picked her up and threw her on the bed. "Bitch I didn't come over here to fuck you. I came over here because I thought you was about to surprise me with some cash. Clearly I was mistaken." I opened the door, ready to leave the room.

"Wait, the money is in my bag over there, on the side of the bed."

I closed the door. "What?"

"You heard me. I said quit your bitching, close the door, and the fucking money is in that Burberry travel bag right there." She pointed with her freshly-manicured nails.

I grabbed the bag and looked inside of it. It was filled with bundles of $100 bills. My eyes lit up. I was so happy I didn't know what to do.

"You know, a thank you would be proper," she said and rolled her eyes.

I smiled at that. "Thank you, baby. I never doubted you for one second," I said, already trying to put together a plan in my head. I had to get my cousin back, and this was my key. Even though I had the money, I knew it was only a part of the equation in getting her back.

Emily climbed out of the bed. "Aren't you going to ask me how I got it all?"

I shook my head. "Nope, just as long as you did."

"Oh, is that right? So, the risks don't matter to you?" she said, grabbing my dick through my pants. I stood back and allowed her to unbutton and unzip my jeans. She fished out my manhood, sucked it into her mouth, and took me deeply down her throat, squeezing my piece like she was trying to squish it. "I had to fuck a senator."

"What?"

"Yeah, he always told me I looked just like his daughter. "She sucked me back into her mouth and moaned.

"What do you mean? If you looked like his daughter, wouldn't that turn him off?"

She took me out of her mouth and licked my tip, sucking my juices from out of the head. "Oh no, that made him want me even more. I've never been fucked so hard by a white man."

She began spearing her head onto my shit so lovely I couldn't help but make a little noise. I didn't quite understand what she was talking about, but everything she was doing to me while she was talking about it felt amazing.

"He said if I spent a night with him and acted like his daughter, he'd pay me 25 grand."

I grabbed a handful of her hair and made her take me to the back of her throat.

"I told him if he doubled it, I'd do anything he wanted."

She stood up and pulled me down on top of her. I fell between her legs with my dick right up against her sex lips. Before I could stop her, she took my pipe and slid it into her hotness. As soon as I got in, I started to kill that shit with all of my might. She screamed at the top of her lungs and begged me to fuck her harder.

"Tell me how you got that money, baby. Tell me how you made it happen for me." I pushed her knees to her chest and long-stroked her, hitting the bottom of her pussy. I had to admit she had a shot on her, and it felt so much better without that rubber on.

"He made me come to his house, and he fucked me in his daughter's bed while I had on her nightgown and panties!" She humped up into my assaults.

I smashed into her even harder. "What else, baby? What else did you do?" I continued to dig deep into her with no mercy. I sped up my pace and bit into her neck.

"He fucked me while I was in her bed, holding her teddy bear. He called me his little girl and said I belonged to him. That made me so wet. It made my pussy squeeze him so tightly. Oh shit! You're fucking my brains out!" she yelled with tears coming down her face.

I had to admit I wasn't taking it easy on her. I picked her up and flipped her over onto her stomach. Grabbing her by the waist, I placed her on all fours and pounded her out so hard I could feel her ass bruising my stomach. She screamed and smashed back into me with velocity. I came when she yelled she was my little girl, and she was coming on my dick.

Afterward, I was getting dressed and ready to get on the mission of rescuing my little cousin when she tried to stop me from leaving. She actually got out of the bed and blocked the door. I was ready to snap. It took all of me to keep my calm.

"Emily, get the fuck away from the door. Stop playing."

"No!"

"Stop playing with me. You know I gotta make shit happen for my people, so move." I tried to move her out of the way, but she would not budge.

"Fuck that, all you want to do is go and hug up with some other bitch."

I felt my temper getting red hot. "Look, I don't got time for this shit. Get yo' punk-ass from in front of the door."

"Punk-ass, really? Now I'm a punk?" She swung at me, trying to slap my face.

"Look, shorty, if you put your hands on me, I'm gon' put mines on you, and you won't like the outcome because I'm tired of playing these games."

She rolled her eyes, still blocking the door. "Look, you aren't leaving out of here anytime soon. I refuse to let that happen, so you might as well take a chill pill."

I took a step back because I was on the verge of busting her in her shit.

"I don't care if you get mad, either, because I just gave you 500 grand, and you can't even spend a night with me? Who the fuck do you think you are?"

I picked the bag of money up and once again walked to the door. "Listen, Emily, let me handle this business and me and you can go on a long vacation afterward. I just want to make sure my cousin is straight."

She exhaled loudly. "What about me, Roman? Why don't you ever worry about how I am doing, huh?" I saw tears rolling down her cheeks.

I grabbed her from the door and wrapped her into my arms. "I do care about you, baby. You just made it happen for me. You're my number one."

"That's not enough!" she whined.

"Emily, what do you want me to do?"

"I want you to love and care about me for real, not only when you need something from me."

I knew what I had to say to her in order to make everything continue to flow properly. "I do love you, and I do care about you more than you know."

"It doesn't seem like it"

"Why is that?"

"Because every time I see you, you're always in need of something. It's never about me. It's always all about you, and that sucks."

"Well, what do you want me to do, Emily? Because clearly you aren't understanding the position I am in."

She shrugged her shoulders. "I don't know. But you can start by staying here all night and making love to me the way you're supposed to."

Now she was starting to get on my nerves. "You know I can't do that tonight. I have to go and make it happen for Alexis. After that, I'm yours."

"So, what if I didn't have the money for you when you came?
Then what?"

"What do you mean?"

"I mean, what if you had come over and I told you I wouldn't have the money until the morning? What would you have done?"

The last thing I wanted to do was sit there and have an argument with this girl about what-ifs. A part of me wanted to grab the bag of money and push her to the side so I could leave out of the door. I needed to get on with the next part of my plans. "Look, Emily, how about I just chill with you for the majority of the night, then at the crack of dawn I'll just go and take care of my business?

That's like the best I can do without risking my people's life. I'm not trying to make it seem like I don't care about you and all that, but now that I got the money, I just want to put an end to all of this. That way I can spend more time with you."

She wrapped her arms around my neck. "And you promise you're going to stay the whole night?"

I nodded. "Yep, and I'm gon' hold you the whole time, too."

I must've been more tired than I thought, because not more than an hour later I was out like a light. I woke up when I felt somebody biting on my neck and a hand going inside my boxers. I opened my eyes to see Emily straddling me and her friend Karen lighting a candle and setting it on the dresser along the vanity.

"Wake up, Roman. I have a surprise for you," she said, leaning down and biting my chest.

I looked to my left and saw Karen lowering her silk nightgown. She stepped out of it and then pulled her panties off of her slim thighs and dropped them to the floor. She stood on the side of the bed, biting on her bottom lip.

"Come on, Emily, I thought you said I was going to be able to get some of his black cock as well. I'm fien'ing for it," she whined. She placed her leg onto the bed, took her hand, and slid it into her sex. Her pussy was shaved bald, the lips a bright pink. Her fingers separated them, exposing her little hole for me to see. "The deal was for her to fuck my dad acting like she was me, get whatever she needed from him money-wise, and in turn I'd be able to have you run your black dick in and out of my tight Irish pussy. I promise you're going to love it, just as long as you hurt me, please." She shoved three fingers up herself and moaned with her head facing the ceiling.

Emily slid down my stomach, positioned my pipe so it sat up against her lips, then she sat on it and began riding me up and down, extending a hand to her friend's pussy. They both played in it, moaning and kissing each other. Karen reached over and squeezed Emily's breasts, pulling on her nipples while Emily finger-fucked a hundred miles an hour while she screamed again and again at the top of her lungs.

"Tell him to fuck me now, Emily. Please make your black man fuck me right now, and tell him to do it hard. Please, I've wanted a black man for so long, and his cock is so freaking big. I need it inside of me." She climbed onto the bed and reached her hand between our legs, playing in our sex juices.

This made Emily slam down onto me even harder. "She wants to fuck you, babe, but it's up to you. Oh shit, just tell me what you want to do!" She rode me faster, moaning with her head tilted backward.

Karen climbed onto the bed and licked my stomach muscles. She squeezed my chest and licked me on the neck. "I want you to put your big black dick inside of me right now. I need you to hurt this pink twat!"

Emily yelled out she was coming and told Karen to rub her vagina's nipple. She must have did it, because all at once Emily began to shake and twitch. "Oh, shit! This dick is so fucking good!" She continued to pump onto me before Karen pushed her off and pulled my pipe out of her. She deep-throated me for a full minute, licking all of Emily's juices from my stalk. She then jumped onto me, forcing me inside of her tight pussy.

I couldn't believe how hot her shit was. It felt like she was on fire. The fit was snug, and the kat was juicy. I grabbed onto her hips and flipped her over. I put her into a ball and fucked her like I hated her. "This what you want, white bitch? Huh? This what you been fantasizing about? You want me to beat this shit open? Well, say no more!" I was ramming her so hard it sounded like somebody was smacking a slab of meat. All I could hear was the sound of me slamming into her box.

"Kill her shit, Roman. Fuck her ass good. I told her you were the bomb. Now she'll know for herself," Emily said, licking all over my back.

I flipped Karen over so she was on all fours. I put that white ass up in the air and spanked her like she was a child. The harder I hit her, it seemed the wetter her pussy got until it was drooling down her leg. This broad was on fire.

"Yes, Roman, fuck the shit out of me! Fuck me until I hate all white men! I love your people!" She screamed and came all over me, back-to-back.

I ended by pulling her hair so hard some strands were left in my palms. I fucked her from the back like I was taking the pussy. Afterward, I watched Emily eat her for all she was worth, then they took turns cleaning me up with their tongues.

T.J. & Jelissa

Chapter 16

Roman

The next morning I woke up at the crack of dawn, and so did they. I had Emily on one side of me with a bowl of fruit, feeding it into my mouth one-by-one, while Karen forked me fried eggs and bacon. I felt good. My dick felt kind of raw, but for the most part I felt like I was ready to get on to the next phase.

I stretched out and yawned. "Yo, last night was killer, but I gotta get going." I looked over to Emily to see what her facial expression would be.

She smiled. "It's okay, baby. Go and handle your business. Just remember you promised when you're done, we're going to take a trip." She licked her lips.

I stood up and started to put my clothes back on. "My word is bond, too."

Karen grunted, "Fuck, you have an awesome body. You must work out every single day. And I want to go with you guys. I just have to get some more of that black dick inside of me. I'll do anything." She sucked her thumb into her mouth and purred.

"Geez, you're such a whore." Emily rolled her eyes. "That's still my man, and don't you have to get things prepared for the Republican National Convention your father placed you in charge of? Aren't all of the Senators supposed to be coming to Chicago this week or whatever?"

"Holy shit, you're right. I bet I have a thousand emails I've missed already." She jumped out of the bed, walked over, and dropped to her knees. She kissed the tip of my penis. .

"I'll worship your black penis forever. I am officially your slave. If ever you need anything from me, you can have it, as long as you promise to fuck the shit out of me like you did last night. Do we have a deal?" she asked, looking up at me with her bright blue eyes.

I smiled.

Emily got out of the bed and pulled her up by her shoulders. "Listen here, Karen. Now, I didn't mind sharing him with you because that was our deal, but that's the end of that. You will not be allowed to fuck my man any longer. He belongs to me, you got that?"

Karen shook her head. " This bitch must really think you guys are still in slavery or something, like she owns you. I'll tell you what, if this was slavery or back in the day and he had a price on him, I'd pay it in a fucking heartbeat. I don't care what the price would have been. Hell, if there's a price now, I'll pay it." She looked at me and winked.

"Whatever that price is, I'll always take care of that for him. He is mine!"

"You must forget my family has double the amount of money as yours. I'll outbid you for him any day, just pick the time and place."

"Get out of my fucking room, Karen, and get off of my property!"

Karen walked, bent over, and started to put her underwear back on. "That's okay, money talks." She got fully dressed, came over, and kissed me on the cheek. "I'll see you soon, Roman. And when I do, I'll be making you an offer you can't refuse."

As soon as Karen left Emily went ballistic. "Well, I see where we stand."

I finished getting dressed and gargled some of her mouthwash on my way out the door. I didn't feel like arguing with her.

It was time to get on my business. I was already feeling guilty because I had wasted the night away. "Yo, I ain't got nothing to say about that. That's your buddy. You was supposed to check that bitch." I grabbed the bag of money off the floor, headed out.

She blocked my path. "I'm sorry, Roman, just please don't fuck with that bitch when I'm not around. I need you, and I can't afford to lose you to her like that, so please don't make me." She wrapped her arms around my legs like a little kid that didn't want her parent to leave the house.

I pried her arms apart. " You don't have to worry about losing me. It's me and you forever, baby. I just gotta go handle this business, and I'll be back." I gave her a kiss on the cheek and left in a haste.

It was raining like crazy outside, so much so that by the time I got to my truck, I was drenched and pissed off. I opened the door and got in and damn near jumped out of my seat from shock, because there in my passenger's seat was Karen, her red hair matted to her forehead, but with a big smile on her face.

"I told you, Roman, that it wouldn't be easy to get rid of me." She whipped her hair behind her back. "Now, listen to me. You are the most gorgeous man I have ever known, and nobody has ever screwed me the way you did all night. I am hooked on you, and I won't stop coming at you until I own a little part of you. So now, listen to me. This here is a phone. I will be contacting you real soon on it. I have already put all of my information on it so you can contact me no matter where I am. There is absolutely nothing you can't have in this world anymore, trust me. All you have to do is ask, and all I'll ever want from you is your cock, that's it. You don't have to involve Emily because she is too insecure. Think things over and let me know whatever you want, and it's yours." She pulled my head to hers, and for the first time in my life I kissed a white girl on the lips.

She jumped out of my truck and climbed into her MBZ S 550. I shook my head, trying to get the cobwebs out just as Ariana's phone buzzed. I picked it up right away, and Jaheim's punk-ass face appeared. He had a cigar in his hand and a bottle of champagne in the other. "What's up, my nigga? I just thought I'd check in on you to see where you at on my bread crumb count."

I didn't have the patience for his rhetoric that morning. "Look, I got your bread right now."

He looked into the camera, shocked. "All of it?"

"Yeah, all of it. Where you wanna meet at? But keep in mind I'm not gon' let you take me for a fool this time. I gotta walk away with my cousin as soon as you get your bread. That's how that has to work."

He looked into the lens, suspicious. "I already told you once you get my paper this time, you could have this bitch, I meant that. Alright then, we gon' meet at the same place at seven in the morning. You bring me my money, and I'll being you your cousin. We'll both leave with what we want." He wagged his finger into the camera. "Now, if there is any funny business, then I promise you it's gon' be an ugly sight for you and her, that's for damn true."

"No funny biz. I just want my people, that's all."

"Well, you most definitely got that coming. Just give me what belongs to me and I'll do the same. Oh, and another thing: bring my daughter with you. I want to see her."

The screen went black. Just as it did, the phone itself rang and I answered it, still Facetiming. Tiny's yellow face entered the screen. She looked like she was worried about something.

I started my truck and drove off into traffic. "Yo, what's the matter with you?" I asked, scared out of my mind.

"I been worried about you. Where have you been at?"

I shook my head. "I been out here taking care of this business like I'm supposed to. How are you doing?"

She ran her fingers through her hair wildly. "That depends on what news you have for me, because I'm going crazy over here worrying about you and Alexis, so tell me something good."

I got onto the expressway and increased my speed just as the rain started to come down even harder. I could barely see, even with my windshield wipers on high. I tried to pay attention and look into her screen as well. "I should be getting Alexis back in the morning. I got all of the bread and I just got off the phone with Jaheim seconds before you called, and we gon' make this happen in the morning."

Tiny started screeching so loud I had to cover my ears.

"Praise Jehovah! Praise God! Oh, He is so good to us! Thank You!" She started to cry. "Roman, I love you so damn much!"

I nodded. "I know, ma, but don't start saying that shit until we got her in our arms, anything before then would be stupid."

"But still, you are the truth. I don't know what I would do without you."

In her background I could see a white arm wrap around her shoulder, and I assumed it was Leah. "Look don't mention it. I just did what I'm supposed to do." I got into the right exit lane, ready to get off on Cottage Grove. I had so many things going over in my mind. The last few weeks had been the craziest of all of my life. I wanted to get my li'l cousin home. I needed to make sure she was safe and sound. I had not even gotten the chance to spend any quality time with her. "Look, Tiny, just chill and I'll be there in a minute."

"Okay, I'll see you when you get here. And just be prepared to have a whole house full of women all over you like you deserve."

I had to laugh at that. "Alright, I got you." I hung up her feed and pulled off of the expressway, trying to make sense of things. I had to find a strategic way to get my li'l cousin back without putting all of my eggs into one basket. I couldn't let Jaheim get the upper hand of me again. There was no way I would be able to come up with the sum of money I had again, so I had to be smart, and I had to leave with her in my arms.

I pulled up to the light, and sat back in my seat, trying to collect my thoughts. My mind was running a mile a minute. I felt fatigued and rundown. I even felt a little sick, like I was about to throw up or something. I looked up at the red light, and it became blurry to me. Before I knew it, I had dozed off for a brief second. I felt my neck going backward, and that jolted me awake. I shook my head and looked up at the light again, and it was turning yellow and then back red. That meant I had snoozed through an entire green light. I had to laugh at that.

The rain started to come down really hard, so much so it sounded like someone was dropping rice on the top of my roof. I could not wait to get home.

I looked down at the phone, preparing to call Tiny back to ask her if she'd cooked anything, when my truck was hit from behind, knocking me forward a little. I looked into the rearview mirror and saw the small Geo Metro's passenger getting out of her car. She flagged me down and pointed to the back of my truck. I was just about to pull off and let matters be when she walked all the way up to my driver's side window and did the "roll your window down" motion with her hand.

I did exactly that and stared into the face of a heavyset woman with a light mustache.

"Hey, I'm sorry, my car slid a little bit. Can I take down your information?"

I shrugged her off. "Is the damage that bad?" She had hit me pretty hard. I mean, for her having a little car, it made my truck jerk forward. I looked into the rearview mirror at the front end of her vehicle. I could barely make it out because of the rain.

"Yeah, it's a bit of a mess. You should probably take a look back here and grab a few pictures for your insurance company. We can also exchange information, that way I can take care of my end of things." She adjusted the hood over her head as the rain continued to come down full blast.

Now, had my mind been thinking clearly, it would have told me this broad ain't have no damn insurance. And if she did, the average person in the hood that rolled around in a Geo Metro damn sure wouldn't be so quick to pay for a mistake they'd made. She just seemed too overly friendly. And like I said before, if my mind would have been functioning properly, I would have picked up on things a lot sooner, but by the time I did, it was too late.

I got out of my truck into the pouring rain, holding a spring jacket over my head as thunder boomed in the sky so loud it made my eardrums ring. I followed the woman to my back bumper to assess the damage.

"You see, I just hit it enough to cause a dent." She knelt down and pointed to just above my bumper.

Lightning lit up the entire sky. I bent down to get a closer look, and that's when it seemed out of nowhere she came from out of her jacket with a gun and slammed it to the bottom of my chin. At the same time, a brown van pulled up on the side of us and four young teens got out with long dreads. Only one of them was armed, and he did most of the talking.

"Break yo'self, fool. Give us everything!" he said, holding the Mossberg pump to the back of my head. "Lay yo' bitch-ass on the ground. Now!"

I felt myself being thrown to the ground, and then the lady from before was checking my pockets roughly.

"Yo, I ain't got no cash on me, but everything I got, you can have. It ain't that serious, homie," I said, already feeling myself ready to throw up.

"Shut up! Take everything. Strip that nigga and take that truck. Let's go!"

All of my clothes were taken off of me. I was literally left in the rain with nothing but my boxers on. I was cold as hell, and I was a long way from my crib. I didn't know what to do. Not only had they taken my truck, but I'd left all of the money right there on my passenger's seat.

Chapter 17

Tiny

After getting off of the phone with Roman, I was beside myself with glee. I kept imagining having my daughter back the next day, and that was causing me to become happily hysterical. I couldn't wait for him to get here. I just wanted to wrap my arms around him and let him know how much I appreciated him on all levels. There was nothing I could accomplish without my cousin.

Leah came into my bedroom, walked over, and gave me a hug.

"Hey, Mom. How are you doing?" she asked, holding on to me.

"I'm okay, baby. I'm waiting for Roman to get home."

She nodded her head. "Oh, is he supposed to be coming soon or something?" she asked, rubbing my back.

I nodded and stood up. "He said he'd be on his way now, so I'm hoping that's the truth. He's supposed to have good news for us regarding Alexis."

Leah's eyes lit up. "Geez, oh really? Wow, what if he brings her with him right now? Wouldn't that be awesome?" she said, hugging me tight.

I had to calm her down because she was getting too riled up. "Well, I don't think it's as good of news as that. But he did say he was getting very close."

Leah's euphoria seemed to fade some. "Oh, well, I guess we'll just wait until he's here, then." She looked defeated. "Before I forget, Jackie said to come downstairs because the food is done, and she's nearly done setting the table.

As hungry as I was, I sat at the table and couldn't bring myself to put a lick of food to my mouth. Jackie had made fried chicken, baked macaroni and cheese, cornbread, and a German Chocolate cake. I was starving, yet I was unable to eat.

She looked across the table at me and smiled. "Ms. Johnson, are you okay?" Jackie asked, pouring juice into her glass, grabbing my glass, and filling it the same way.

"Yeah, I'm okay, baby. I just don't seem to have an appetite. My head is spinning like crazy, you know."

Leah stood up. "Mom, do you want me to go and get you some aspirin?"

I shook my head. "No, thank you. It's not one of those head things, to be honest."

"Oh."

"Well, if you want, Ms. Johnson, I can put your food up and then reheat it when you're better?"

I nodded. "Yeah, I think that will be best for right now, honey. At least until I can get a better hold on myself."

I slid my chair away from the table.

Leah stood up, carrying her plate. "Mom, is there anything I can do to make you feel better?"

"No, baby, just go back to the table and eat your food. I need some time alone with my thoughts."

She looked a little hurt. She turned around with her head down, and walked back into the dining room. "Okay, but holler if you need me."

I had so many things going through my mind. I couldn't wait until I'd be able to sit down with Roman so I could let him know everything that had taken place. I needed to hear his perspective on King and Chris and how we should handle them. Me personally, I felt like after it was all said and done, we would have to worry about Chris. I felt like he had something up his sleeve, or he was still harboring a grudge toward me for what took place nearly 18 years prior. I knew he didn't care about getting Alexis back, that was for damn sure, and neither did King. All they cared about was Prince, which I understood because quiet as kept, all I cared about was my daughter and getting her home safe and sound.

I heard the front door slam. "Fuck, that son of a bitch has had somebody else flag me down trying to offer me money. He's up to a hundred grand. I nearly took it just so he'd leave me the hell alone," Ariana said, putting her umbrella away.

I came down the stairs slowly. "Who are you talking about, baby?"

"Noah. He just had some freaking Jewish guy in a Benz roll up on me and Rosie while we were in the cell phone shop. The guy pulled me to the side and said he'd give me a hundred grand to drop the charges against Noah. He wants me to recant my entire story."

Rosie came in with her pink umbrella. "Yo, momma, I don't know what you're thinking, but that was a hundred racks. I would have taken that in a heartbeat. I mean, why not?"

Ariana looked over to me. "Because my mother said it's not a good idea and we have bigger fish to fry with him, right Mom?"

I came over to the front entrance with a mop and proceeded to mop up all the water from the rain outside what they'd brought in with them. "That's right, baby. If he's willing to offer you a hundred grand, the courts will be willing to give you ten times that. The son of a bitch shouldn't have put his filthy hands on to you. Now he has to pay."

Rosie put her hand on her hip. "Wait a minute, I thought you said you gave him the pussy."

Ariana blushed. "I did at first, but then I told him to stop and he kept on going."

Rosie smiled. "Sounds like some good sex to me, but I don't know, I guess I'm just new wave. *Sabes que*, I tell a man yes and then no and he takes it from me anyway. That just means he loves what I have to offer, that I'm a hot *mamita*, *si moan!*" She ran her tongue over her lips and growled. "When he got money like that, all you gotta do is point him out to me, and he can get this *chocha* right now, in front of everybody. He can wire the hundred grand later, but in that moment he'd get the best of Mexico!" She started to do some sort of loud tribal call.

I started to crack up because this little Mexican girl was off her rocker. "Baby, don't listen to her. She's clearly crazy. We have to follow the game plan."

The next thing that happened was almost too much. There was a loud beating on the door that scared everybody in the house. I mean, we all ran up the stairs, damn near tripping over each other. And if that wasn't bad, then there was a loud boom from the thunder and all the lights went out in the house. The banging started again, and I didn't know what to do.

"Somebody go answer the door," Ariana said, holding onto my arm.

"Yeah, somebody go see who it is," Rosie whispered, hiding behind me at the top of the stairs.

"Rosie, why don't you go?" Ariana asked. I could feel her shaking on my arm.

"Me? Why should I go? This ain't my house, and plus I'm Latina. We're just like you black folks: we never go toward the danger; we go away from it. *Sabes que*, I'm about to go and find a window." She looked serious. "Hey, why don't you go, Leah? You're white." "What does that have to do with anything?" she whined.

Rosie shrugged her shoulders. "Just saying that in the movies, the white girls always go toward the danger. Just thought you'd like to get a jump on your acting career."

"Yeah, you should go, Leah. Besides, who's braver than you here?" Jackie chimed in.

"Ariana should go, she's not afraid, besides she's always talking about death and everything anyway."

"Well, looks like she has a point, *mami*." Rosie nudged Ariana in the direction of the front door just as the loud banging returned and the lights in the house popped back on.

Ariana shrugged her shoulders. "Okay, I'll go, but I just think it's sad how you guys used my personal struggles I told you about against me. That's just wrong, man." She slowly made her way down the stairs.

"Stop, baby, I'm going. Get your butt back up these stairs and y'all go in the room, now!" I yelled.

"No, Mom, I'm going with you. You are not answering that door alone. It's not happening," Leah said, coming to stand beside me.

Rosie sighed, "Well, there you have it. You got two people to answer the door instead of one. Yo, Ms. Johnson, I had your back and all, but I ain't trying to step on Leah's toes, so y'all handle that business down there and I'll see what's happening under the bed. Gotta make sure ain't no monsters under there or nothing, nah mean?"

She ran into the room. "This is scarier than the cartel in Mexico."

The loud banging persisted. "Who is it?" I asked. I could hear a muffled voice on the other end, but I couldn't make it out clearly. "Who is it?" I asked again, walking closer to the door.

Leah stepped forward and peeked out of the window. "Oh my god, it's Roman!" She ran to open the door.

Why would Roman be knocking on the door when he had his own key? What was going on? My mind started to spin super fast, so much so I got dizzy. Once she opened the door and I saw him run in wearing only his boxers, which were matted to him because of the rain, I'd had all that I could take. I fainted.

When I awoke, he was holding me in his arms with tears in his eyes. I had to blink twice to allow my vision to focus because I was seeing two of him. My head was still spinning. My tongue tasted like I had thrown up, and I would later find out I had.

"They stripped me, cuz. Them muthafuckas caught me slipping and took all of the fucking money, every penny!" The tears streamed from his eyes and dripped down to his chest.

"What are you talking about? You just told me everything was good." I tried to sit up and noted we were in my bedroom. He was seated on the couch with me laid in his lap.

He nodded. "Yeah I know, but I was on my way home when some bitch bumped me with her car. I got out to see how much damage was done, and that's when they robbed me. They took my truck, my phones, and the cash, all 500 thousand of it!" He sat up and placed me so I was sitting on the couch alone while he paced back and forth.

"Fuck!" He slammed his hand into his forehead again and again.

"Roman, calm down. Getting yourself riled up ain't gon' do nothing but make the situation worse. We just have to use our heads to find another solution." I sounded way more optimistic than I actually was because inside I was panicking and starting to imagine something severe happening to my daughter. I was about to freak out.

He shook his head. "Tiny, you don't understand. Once I got the money, that fool Jaheim hit me up and I told him that I'd meet with him tomorrow and I'd have his cash in full. How the hell am I going to meet up with him? And I'm supposed to have his cash in full. He made that perfectly clear. There is also something else." At saying this he ran his hand over his bald head and shook it. "Now he wants to see Ariana. He made that a part of the deal, and before I could say anything, he wound up killing the feed. So, what are we going to do?"

Now things were getting rough. We didn't have any money to give this man, and on top of that, he was talking about wanting my other daughter, whom I had sworn to protect for the rest of my life. I had a feeling he was going to try to pull a switch-a-roo. I couldn't let that happen. There was no telling what he'd do to Ariana once he got her. "I don't know, but we can't allow him to get his hands on her."

"We have to come up with some sort of plan by the morning or something might happen to my little cousin, and I will never be able to live that down."

"I know, and I know you've been doing all you can for her. Stop being so hard on yourself. You have to think positive, because that's all we can do."

Rosie stepped into the room very slowly. "Hey, did you tell him about King and Chris?" She came and sat close to me on the couch.

"King and Chris? What the fuck they got to do with anything?" he boomed as if he were about to snap out.

"Yo, *papi*, I don't know. Maybe you should talk to your cousin right here, because I ain't got nothing to do with it." Rosie said, getting as far away from him as possible. She looked terrified. "Yo, first you're beating on the door, now this. I can't let you beat on my ass, *sabes que*? My family needs me." She stood and watched us from the other side of the room.

I was frozen in place, looking at this girl because she was something else. I didn't know what to do with her. "Roman, calm down and let me explain."

"Fuck all of that. Do you have any idea what them dudes did to my mother when I was little?" He punched through the air and sat down with his hands covering his face.

I came over and rubbed his back. "I don't know, and maybe you should tell me, that way I can."

"They forced her to inject that poison into her veins. They turned my mother into a heroin addict, and ever since then she ain't been right."

"What do you mean they forced her?" I asked, sitting beside him.

Rosie took out a candy bar and peeled back the wrapper with her eyes wide open as if she were extremely interested. The other girls came into the room and sat on the floor beside her. They looked to me to make sure it was okay. I nodded my head.

"When I was about 16 years old, a nigga named Draylon used to run the whole Robert Taylor Homes where we stayed. He was a fool that come up from our buildings. He was a hustler, and he repped our turf. He made sure everybody respected our projects. Most of the times he went to war, it was because of niggas trying to take over our buildings just so they could take advantage of our people." He stood up and began to pace the floor.

"So, what happened to him, and where does King come in at?" Rosie said, opening a bag of popcorn. She looked like she was ready for him to spill the tea.

He gave her a look to say he thought she was crazy.

"Anyway, I grew up with them niggas, King and Chris. They were a little older than me, but I was around enough to see how they got down. King used to sell dope for Draylon when he was just a young teen. From what I could see, he always treated him good and made sure he was well taken care of. King pledged his loyalty to Draylon, and even killed niggas for him. Then one day Draylon got murdered, and that's when things took a turn for the worse. That fool King wound up sending his own troops to raid the projects, and in the mist of all of that, they kicked in apartment doors, and any adult that was present, they shot heroin into them. And I ain't talking no regular run-of-the-mill heroin. I'm talking about that some chemically-enhanced shit that made everybody that got shot up crazy over that drug. It took over their lives. It got so bad that them niggas pretty much became gods overnight because people worshipped them – and still do – over that damn drug."

"So, what happened to your mom?" Ariana asked with tears in her eyes.

"Somebody from dude's crew injected her with that poison , and my mother been addicted to it every since. She can only last a few weeks out of rehab at a time."

"Yo, that's messed up, man. I can see now why you were punchin' at the air and stuff. You kinda felt like Trey from *Boys in the Hood*, huh?"

He looked at her like she'd lost her mind. "So, tell me what's good with these fools now?"

Tiny cleared her throat. "Well, that's sort of a tough act to follow." I shook my head. "Okay, do you remember I told you on the day I got locked up for that murder I was supposed to be dropping off a large sum of money to somebody?" I turned to look at him.

His eyes bugged out of his head. "You was talking about them niggas!"

I shook my head. "No, I wasn't talking about the both of them. I was just talking about Chris. You see, Alexis' father had brought some dude into their fold who started to steal from King and Chris, and Chris made him pay the dude's debt. Chris snatched us up and said the only way he would let us go free was if we paid back what that dude had stolen. Long story short, I was on my way to paying that debt before they locked me up bogusly for that murder."

"So, you're saying you still owe this fool and that's why they been hounding you?"

"No, papi, let her finish. You keep interrupting the story. That's very rude of you. Where are your manners?" Rosie said, looking serious.

"The boy Alexis went missing with is King's son. King has put up a million-dollar reward for information leading to the safe return of his son. They are trying to track Jaheim down, and I am guessing if they got chips like that, it won't be long before they do."

Roman waved his hand through the air. "Yo, them niggas is super selfish, though. I can't see them giving a

178

fuck about Alexis enough to rescue her, too. Once they get their kid, they ain't gon' think twice about blowing that whole block up. That's with her still on it. Trust me, I done witnessed these fools in action before. They ain't nothing nice."

"So, what are you saying?" I asked, completely defeated.

"I'm saying we gotta come up with our own plans, and we gotta get her back before they find him, because once they do, Jaheim is going to die, and Alexis will be caught in the crossfire. We need to get in touch with this fool and set up a new date or something, because he's expecting me to be there tomorrow with his money and his daughter."

Roman tried to catch himself at the end. We both shot glances at Ariana. She looked shocked and confused. Slowly, she stood up and watched us carefully.

"With me? So, when were you guys going to tell me about this?" she asked with her voice beginning to crack.

"Baby, it's not what you think. We were just…"

"Just what? Going to trade me off so you can get your precious daughter back? And in the meantime I take her place, right?"

"Nobody said anything about you taking her place, or us giving you to him at all. I was just saying what he expected, that's all."

"When were you guys going to tell me this, though? Clearly you've had this knowledge for some time now, so why am I just hearing about it?"

"Aw, snap! It's about to go down up in here. Y'all better tell sister-girl what's good. *Sabes que*, she's turning red and everything," Rosie said, shaking her head.

"I just found out about this when Roman got home. We were trying to figure out how we would get around that aspect of things."

"But when were you going to tell me this, though? Like, this is my whole life we're talking about right now."

"We haven't even had time to process that information, Ariana. You need to calm down because you're only adding fuel to the fire. There is no need to rile yourself up. We're not going to let anything happen to you," I said, rubbing my temples. I was getting a migraine headache, and my vision das becoming hazy.

"You know what you sound like? Do you? You sound like a freaking politician trying to avoid answering a question or something. I asked you when were you going to tell me about this, and you have still not given me an answer." She smashed her fist into her hand. "Don't you know that if he got to Alexis, he can get to me just as easily, especially if my own freaking family isn't watching over me the day I thought they were?"

She took her jacket and yanked it out of the closet. "I can't believe this crap. Here I am thinking I'm safe and sound, and all along you guys are using me as bait. Life sucks!" she yelled and slammed her coat to the floor.

Leah got up to try to comfort her. "Ariana, we all love you so much. You have to know that."

Ariana pushed her away. "Fuck you. All you care about is sniffing her fucking feet, and you're so obsessed with my sister you've made our mother yours. You don't hear Jackie calling her that shit. News flash, she's not your mother. She's ours. Bitch, you're white. Go and find your own mother."

"Ariana!" I began.

"Crap, hey, I'm sorry, Leah! I didn't mean it." She tried to put her arm around Leah.

Leah dropped to the floor and cried her eyes out. "I'm sorry, Ariana. I just love you guys so much, and she's the best mother I have ever had."

Ariana dropped to the floor and placed her arms around her. "I know, me too."

It took us the whole night in order to get a full understanding. In order for everything to work, we would all have to do our parts, and we would have to trust each other and know we each had each other's best interests at heart. Our sole dilemma was the fact the phone Jaheim contacted us on had been stolen in the robbery, so we didn't know how we were going to reach out to him. There was also the fact we did not have his money, or any number close to that amount.

We had to come up with a good plan, and fast.

T.J. & Jelissa

Chapter 18

Roman

"I didn't expect you to call me so suddenly. To what do I owe this pleasure?" Karen asked, leaning over the seat and kissing my lap.

"Last night when I left here, I got robbed on the south side of Chicago. They took the phone you gave me, my own, and $500,000 in cash."

She bucked her eyes and sat back in her seat. "Well, at least you're okay."

"That's true, but my little cousin isn't. Now, that money was to be used to pay her ransom. She was abducted nearly a week ago, and ever since then I've been trying to come up with that money. Emily came through for me, and now it's lost. I need your help."

She looked off into space, then licked her lips. "So, what are you saying? Are you saying I'm going to be able to get some more of this cock?" She reached between my legs and squeezed my dick hard. "You tell me you're going to fuck my brains out and I'll do anything you need me to do. Money is only money, right?" She unzipped my jeans and snaked her hand inside of them, feeling hot skin with her thumb. She trailed it across my head.

"That's not all. I gotta have this money by the morning. That's the deadline, and there is no way around it. Can you make it happen?" I felt her pull my piece out and wrap her hot mouth around it.

"That depends on how they want it. If they want it wired, I'll do it right now and have it sent in five minutes. If they want cash, we can go to my uncle's bank in about two hours or so. Just give me enough time to go over and do what I need to do to him and he'll give me the key to the safe. It won't hurt him any, trust me." She popped me back into her mouth and sucked me like she was trying to prove a point.

I fucked her for the next hour straight with all of my might. I tried to break her back. By the time I was finished, she had tear streaks all over her face, and her makeup was barely there. I had also managed to pull out a nice portion of her extensions.

I paced back and forth in her room, waiting on her to get back with the money. I had to admit I was paranoid. I felt like something wasn't right, but then again, so far what had been? I tried to eat a slice of the pizza she left out for me but every time I put it to my mouth, I got sick. Finally, at about three in the morning, she came and handed me a folder with five hundred $1,000 bills. Before that point, I didn't even know they existed.

"Here you go, baby, just like I promised. Now, tell me you don't need that bitch anymore. Tell me I'm the only white bitch you'll ever need." She wrapped her hands around my waist and started biting my neck.

"I see you make shit happen, baby. Why would I need anybody other than you?" I said, stuffing the bills in my bag.

"That's what I like to hear. I like to hear you're mine, so tell me that one time, please!"

I knew this broad was off her rocker, but if that's what she needed to hear, then I had no problem telling her that. "I'm yours, baby."

She lay down on the bed and opened her legs, pulling her panties to the side. "Tell me I own you. That you're my slave, baby."

I decided to play into her fantasy. "I'm your slave, white woman."

She moaned. "Yes, tell me more."

"All of this black skin is yours to do whatever with that you please."

"Yes, please, more," she said, digging her fingers into her deeply.

"I'm here for you to beat me until I bleed, white woman."

"Yes! Oh shit, yes!" I could hear her fingers slurping in and out of her now.

"I want you to beat me and make me put this big, black African dick inside of your pink twat."

"Yes!"

"I take your cunt and fuck you until you bleed, and then I'm gon' fuck you some more."

She humped off the bed into her hand. Her fingers were like blurs going in and out of her now. "Oh please, fuck me now. Need you to hurt my pussy until I can't walk anymore!"

And that's just what I did until she passed out a few times. Each time I woke her back up by treating her ass rough as I could. I tossed her all over that bedroom. I fucked her up against the wall, on top of her dresser, on the floor, in her closet, up against her bedroom door, and in every hole I could fit into. When it was all said and done, she was out like a light.

We awoke three hours later, it seemed at the same time. The first thing on my mind was meeting with Jaheim. I didn't even know how I was going to get into contact with him because I no longer had that phone, and I told her that.

"Oh, don't worry about that. Just give me the number to that old phone."

I did. I watched her leave the room and come back into it with a laptop.

"You see, what I am going to do is shut that other phone off, and I'm going to reactivate your number with this one right here. That way, when he contacts you this morning, the feed will come to this one and no one will be the wiser. I'll teach you a few things along the way, don't worry." She smiled while she worked. The scent of her pussy was all through the air in the room.

"I see I made the best choice in you, then, huh?"

She licked her lips. "I don't know, you tell me?"

I had to laugh at that comeback, especially when she opened her legs and spread her sex lips. I guess she was trying to tell me she knew her pussy was better than Emily's, and to be honest, it really was.

No sooner than when she switched the phone lines up did Jaheim's ugly face appear, letting me know he wanted to Facetime. I was glad it happened when it did because Karen was right there to verify all of this shit was real. I made her stand back out of the camera shot, though.

He went right in on me. "What's up, fuck-nigga? You got my money this morning, or am I bodying this bitch and getting on with my day? He lit a cigar and blew the smoke into the camera.

"Yeah, I got your bread, homie. Everything should be squared away today. I don't want no funny business. All I want is my people back."

"You can definitely get her ass back. I think she sick or some shit. She been throwing up and not eating at all, so pretty much if you don't come and get her, she probably gon' drop dead anyway."

186

I felt myself getting ready to panic. "What are you talking about?"

He shrugged his shoulders. "Just like I said."

"Man, what's the matter with her?"

"Nigga, I ain't no muthafucking doctor, and I ain't about to take her to one. My job about to be done today. I'm tired of this stubborn-ass bitch. She gotta go, one way or the other. I mean that shit!"

I nodded. "Alright, bruh. Well, I got your paper, and I made shit easy. I got you all $1,000 bills." I flashed them into the camera.

"What the fuck you know about $1,000 bills, nigga, huh?" He took a puff of his cigar. "Let me find out you done went and robbed a bank vault or something. I mean, I don't give a fuck as long as at the end of the day my shit spends."

"Well, you definitely won't have no problem with that." I ran my hand over my head, noting for the first time it needed to be shaved again. "Yo, Jaheim, let me see her, boss. I mean, just for a few seconds." I could tell he was back in some dungeon because there was nothing but concrete around him.

"You know what, since I'm feeling in an okay mood, I'm gon' let you have that." He stepped out of one room, and in the background I could see a bunch of masked people around him. He got to a door and took a combination lock off, then pushed it in. I saw Alexis right away, curled into a corner with her knees to her chest.

"Your cousin on the feed."

She picked her head up and faced the phone. "Hey, Roman. Are you coming to get me?"

"You'll be coming home today, in a few hours."

She seemed out of breath. "I can't wait. That's going to be so cool."

"I know, baby, so just hold on."

"Roman, when you get here, can you take me to get something to eat? Because I'm starving worse than ever."

I nodded with tears running down my cheeks. "Yeah, ma, we can get whatever you like, I promise. All I need for you to do is to hold on and keep fighting."

Jaheim snatched the camera away from her. "And bitch-nigga, all I need you to do is to have my paper! Beat me there, don't meet me there."

Behind him I could see Alexis struggling to keep her head up. She looked weak and drained, as if she was barely alive. On top of that, the room she was being kept in looked cold. I watched her shake with the shivers, and at least I prayed it was from the cold and not from anything else that could be harmful to her health.

"I'll be there, don't you worry about that."

***

Ariana

My head was all screwed up. There was something about walking in on their conversation and hearing them discuss taking me off as part of the ransom that was doing something to me. I wasn't feeling like a part of the family. I was feeling like a pawn within their grand scheme of things.

I paced back and forth in my room, unsure of what I wanted to do with my day. I knew that basically the whole family was preparing for the return of my sister, and I guess on a normal front I should have been just as happy as they were, but I just wasn't.

I looked out of the window to see my mother and Jackie load up into one of Roman's friend's cars before pulling away from the curb. As soon as they did, I slumped down to the floor and bawled my eyes out. I cried because I knew things were about to change drastically. Once my sister got back home, I knew I would be an afterthought to my mother, and the small ounce of love I was shown would be stripped away.

Rosie came into the room eating a bowl of cereal. She was crunching so loud I could tell she didn't have much milk on it.

"Damn, *mamita*, you looking all sad and shit. What's the matter?" She came over and sat on the bed.

I ran my fingers through my hair in an attempt to keep from screaming. Rolling my head around on my shoulder, I took a deep breath and exhaled loudly. "I don't know, I am just feeling some type of way." I placed both hands around the back of my neck and continued to roll my neck.

" You know, I ain't no shrink or nothing, but I think you're freaking out because you're going to meet your father today for the first time, and it scares you. You're probably thinking he might hurt you or something, or maybe you're thinking he might keep you." She shrugged her shoulders. "He sounds pretty screwed up to me."

For some reason that comment stung me, and I took offense to it. "Rosie, just don't, okay?" I turned to look out the window and noted it was going to be another rainy day. It was already starting to drizzle from the sky. Though it was early in the morning, it was still dark out. The atmosphere seemed a little cool.

Rosie continued to eat her cereal. "You know, if my father was as crazy as yours, I don't know what I'd do. I know I'd never want to meet him, though. Kidnapping people, tying them up, and demanding ransoms? *Sabes que,* he sounds like the freaking cartel back in my country." She got up from the bed and left the room.

As she walked out, Leah came in and walked over to me, rubbing my back. "Are you okay in here?" She knelt down beside me, looking me in the face.

"No, I'm not, Leah. I feel like shit, and I don't know why." I bounced up and began to pace the floor. I was starting to feel angry. "You know, I wonder how all of you must look at me. I mean, you know my mom committed suicide, and my father is clearly out of his mind, so I wonder what you guys say about me when I'm not around." I continued to pace back and forth, my blood pressure rising.

Leah shook her head. "What's gotten into you? This is supposed to be a joyous day. Why are you up here acting as if you're pissed Alexis is coming home?" She said this while looking at me from the corner of her eye.

"You know what? I'm so tired of hearing my sister's name that if I hear it again, I swear I'm going to snap out." I took another deep breath, pausing in my tracks to do so. "There has to be more to life than Alexis."

At hearing this, Leah stood up and nearly blocked my path of pacing. "What did you just say about my best friend?" she asked, zooming in on me, her face turning a shade of pink.

I stopped pacing and walked right into her face. "I said there has to be more to life than Alexis. Now, do you have a problem with that?"

She lowered her head and shook it slowly. I could tell she was trying to control her anger. "No, I don't, but you should, because that's your sister. You're so freaking selfish that it's making somebody as beautiful as you completely ugly. Get a hold of yourself." She turned to walk away just as Rosie came back into the room.

She scolded, "Wow, Ariana. I see your true colors, and they are ugly. A person could never tell just by looking at you, but you are sick." She left the room.

That was all it took the break the camel's back. I had it up to the roof with their nonchalant comments about me. I was so sick and tired of people judging me and looking at me differently. I didn't like, nor did I care about either one of those girls. Who were they to judge me and to try to make me feel less human? So what if my parents were a little weird? That didn't mean I was an alien, although I couldn't deny I hated myself. I hated the blood that flowed through my veins, and I wish I would have been born under different circumstances. But I wasn't, and I couldn't change who I was or how I'd gotten here.

One thing I could change was how those bitches standing outside of my bedroom treated me, though. I went out into the hallway where they were standing and smiled. They looked at me like I was crazy, and I probably was getting there. "Hey, guys, I'm sorry. It's just that today Roman is going to use me as a pawn to get my sister back, and I was a little on edge about that. I didn't think it was fair, so I wound up saying some things I really didn't mean. I just hope you guys can understand that's all it was and forgive me, because I really didn't mean anything by it."

They stood at the top of the stairs, facing me. Leah nodded, and smiled warmly. "It's okay, Ariana. We know you are going through a lot, and we are here for you. I'm not going to turn my back on you because I can only imagine how rough things must be for you." She walked over to me and wrapped me within her arms.

Rosie came over and did the same. "Look, *mami*, you're good. You just gotta stop all of this bipolar shit. One minute you're up, and the next you're down. *Sabes que*, I'm confused, but I got you, though. And when Alexis gets here, she'll have you, too. That's for sure." She squeezed me a little tighter.

I don't know why I did what I did, but a part of me simply lost control of my own will. I don't know if it was because I got to imagining Alexis being there and the whole house turning on me, or if I was just simply sick of waking up to each day and it being all about her and her day. Or maybe it was the fact I knew nobody would go to great lengths to pay my ransom if I had one the way they were going through it for hers. Either way, I waited until our embrace ended and the girls turned around to go down the stairs before me. As soon as they walked to the top, I took a step back and, with all of my might, I pushed them both down the stairs.

Leah flew first, flying with so much velocity she hit her head on the banister and did a complete forward flip, while Rosie tried to balance herself, twisted her ankle first, and fell backward, hitting her head on nearly every step until she hit the bottom. Leah landed with a thud, her neck bent awkwardly.

I stood at the top with my chest heaving up and down. I felt powerful. I looked down on them and saw Leah was unmoving, her eyes wide open, looking into space while Rosie tried to get up. I made my way down the steps.

"Oh, this is some bullshit, here. This bitch done threw me down some stairs and fucked me up. Oh shit, my ankle and my back feel broken. What did I do to deserve this?" she said to herself more than anyone else.

I was in a zone. At that moment I hated the both of them, and I wanted them dead. I no longer wanted them breathing, and the fact they were was causing me to become hysterical. I circled around Rosie as she tried to crawl and regain her composure. "I don't like you, and I know you don't like me, so let's stop faking the funk," I said through clenched teeth.

She continued to crawl, and then abruptly fell to her stomach. "Look, *mami*, I don't have nothing against you. I thought we were cool as snowflakes. You're just tripping right now. I got your back, girl." I noticed the traces of blood corning from her mouth. She seemed out of breath. "Help me," she said before falling on her stomach.

I stepped over her and into the kitchen, grabbing a skillet. I came back into the living room and stood over Leah. She lay with her eyes wide open, her neck all the way to one side of her shoulders, with a bone threatening to stick through her neck.

"It's your fault, too, Leah. You and your greediness of my mother, always sniffing her up. You deserved to die!" I leaned down and started to beat her with the skillet over her head until my arm went tired.

I blacked out, and when I came back to myself, it looked like I had spilled spaghetti sauce all over her face. I turned to look at Rosie, whose eyes were so big they looked as if they were about to fall out of her head. She tried to get onto her knees to crawl again, but could not muster up the strength.

"*Por favor*, please, *mamita*. Don't do that to me, please. I–"

Before she could even finish her sentence, I was beating her over the head with the same skillet, again and again. I was so tired of being different. I was tired of hearing about her perfect family in Mexico, and I was tired of hearing how much she loved Alexis. I was tired of it all.

I brought it down onto her head again and again, feeling her warm blood splatter onto my face. Her body leapt off the ground again and again, but I didn't care. I beat her skull until it was literally mush, then dropped the skillet and looked them both over.

Both were completely dead, there was no doubt about it. They were as dead as my mother. That made me laugh. Now they were actually dead and I had killed them. I started to feel strong. I felt like I finally understood what would make me happy in life, and the answer was to make everybody else unhappy, that way we would all be on the same level, all the time.

I dragged them down to our basement one-by-one, and once down there, I covered their bodies with blankets. I didn't know what else to do with them at that time. They both continued to bleed profusely, saturating the blankets, but I didn't care.

I went back upstairs and mopped up all of the traces of the incident and washed the skillet and put in back in place. I looked around the house, and nothing seemed to be out of place.

I went into the kitchen and made me some breakfast because my stomach was growling and I could eat.

Chapter 19

Tiny

We had everything set in motion, now all we had to do was go get Ariana and bring her to the drop, but that was the part I was worrying about the most. I didn't know what Jaheim had in mind for her, but I could only imagine it would be something horrendous. He had been sick since the day I met him. I'd witnessed him do some pretty heinous things to people while we were in the streets. I remember one girl that used to work with us, he made her eat a shit sandwich and drink a cup full of his piss. There was another girl he'd beat so bad he shattered her eye socket. I also remembered all of the times he'd beat me and then force me to do things I didn't want to do, so I could only imagine over the years he'd gotten worst.

Roman drove on in silence. He was biting on his bottom lip and nodding his head to the Project Kid track that boomed from the speakers. He looked as if he was determined to make things happen. I could tell he was in his own world because I had called his name twice, and he had yet to answer me.

I leaned forward and turned down the music. "Roman, you don't hear me talking to you?" I asked, giving him a crazy look.

He frowned. "Aw, nall, what did you say?" He drove through the green light and increased the speed of the truck.

"I said you've been awfully quiet. What's on your mind?" I reached to the side of me and clicked my seatbelt into place. The rain came down a little harder, and the last time he tried to stop, the car slid a little bit.

He exhaled. "To be honest, I'm just hoping everything goes as planned. I'm ready for Alexis to be home and safe. All I do is think about her, all day long. I'm gon' kill that nigga if he hurt her in any way."

I reached over and squeezed his hand. "Don't even think about nothing like that. Today is going to be a good day. We're going to get her back and be reunited as a family. We'll bring her home and get her clean, then afterward I'm gon' cook her a meal so big she'll bust."

He laughed. "Well, don't do that. We need her around for a little while."

I smiled this time. "But you know what I mean. Everything will work out for the greater good. Jehovah sees, and He has us, you better believe that."

I looked out the windshield and up toward the sky and silently prayed. *Father I know you hear all things, and you see all things. On this day I just pray you allow for my baby to be returned home safe to us. She's suffered for my sins long enough. Please bring her home, Father, and allow for us to be able to live a normal and happy life. In Jesus' name I pray. Amen.*

"I'm worried about this whole Ariana thing, too," Roman said. He'd obviously been talking to me the whole time I was praying, but I had tuned him out.

"Yeah, me too. The reason I am worried is because I think he's going to try and keep her with him in exchange for Alexis, and if that's the case, then what do we do?" I looked him over to see what his facial expression would be.

He shrugged his shoulders. "To be honest with you, all I care about is Alexis. I mean, I got a little love for Ariana, but my heart is my little cousin's. I'm doing all of this for you and for her. Now, I know she is technically your daughter and you made a promise to her mother and all, but, my li'l cousin is my only concern, and I don't even feel bad about that."

Now I exhaled loudly. That didn't help me out one bit, because I was starting to feel guilty. There was no question at all that I loved Ariana. She was my daughter just as well as Alexis, and there was nothing I wouldn't do for her. But just keeping things all the way one hundred, there was nobody on this earth I wouldn't trade in to get Alexis back. Nobody.

"To be honest, I don't know what you're going to do, because you know he's going to try and keep that girl. And if he does, I'm snatching up Alexis and bouncing. That's gon' be that. She's had enough, and besides all of that, she is technically his daughter, so that's some family shit they gotta deal with."

***

When we got back to the house, Ariana was waiting on the couch with her coat on. She saw us and stood up, ran over, and hugged me. " I've missed you, Mommy. I was worried about you like crazy. You too, Roman," she said, looking over my shoulder. "Hey, where is Jackie?"

I shook my head. "She's out with that A'Jhani character. Said she'll be back later on tonight. And I've missed you, too, baby. Are you ready to get this over with?" I wrapped my arms around her and squeezed her tightly.

"I think so," she whispered. "I just hope he doesn't hurt me. I have not done anything wrong to anybody." Her bottom lip began to quiver.

Roman came over and kissed her on the forehead. "Yo, I ain't gon' let nothing happen to you. Far as we know, all he wants to do is see you. He didn't say anything about trading you off or taking you anywhere, so if that comes up, we'll have a problem, and I ain't going." He frowned and clenched the muscles in his jaw. "Let's get this show on the road, though. Where is Leah?"

She shrugged her shoulders. "The last time I saw her, she and Rosie were getting into a car with somebody."

"Did you recognize the car?" I asked.

"No, but then again, Chris is always driving a new car."

"Yeah, you're right about that. Hopefully they are okay and will be here when we get back. Okay, let's roll out."

***

Roman

I pulled the truck into the same spot I had a few days ago, and we waited for him to hit us up. Our scheduled meeting was supposed to be in an hour, but I had gotten there early enough to collect my thoughts. I just couldn't let this event slip through my fingers again. I needed Alexis home so I could ensure she was safe every single night and day. I had not had a good night's sleep ever since I found out she had been taken. I needed it to all be over.

Tiny reached over and squeezed my thigh again. "Hey, it's going to be okay. Don't worry, we got this."

She turned around in her seat to address Ariana. "Look, baby, I love you, and I need you to know that.

You're my daughter and there is nothing in this world I wouldn't do for you. I hate that we are in this position, but it is times like this that will make our family that much stronger. You are a part of me. Don't you forget that." She reached and pulled her close and kissed her on her lips.

"Thank you, Mommy, and I love you, too. I know we have to do this, and I'm okay with it. I will do anything for my sister. I love her with all of me." She kissed her again and rubbed her earlobes. "You're so beautiful. You're the perfect mother." She said this with tears in her eyes.

I didn't know what to say. I felt like they were having a moment, so I just fell back and listened to the rain pelt down on top of the truck loudly. "Y'all stop all that sappy shit. We gon' be alright."

Just then the phone vibrated, and I pulled up Jaheim's image.

"What it do, bitch-nigga?" He pulled Alexis into the shot and placed his arm around her. "Are you in place, or am I whackin' this bitch today?" He pushed her to the ground and I heard her yelp.

"I'm already here and waiting for you, homie." I tried to take my mind off the fact he'd just pushed my cousin to the ground as if she weren't nothing at all.

"So, what all do you have?" he asked, lighting a cigar.

"I got your 500 bands, just like you asked me. What more do you want?"

He laughed. "Oh, I see we about to have a major problem in this muthafucka. Nigga, where is my daughter? I want her, too. Fuck that money if you ain't got her!"

"Yo, chill, nigga. She's right here in the backseat. Say something, Ariana." I held the phone in front of her face.

"Hey, Dad, how are you doing?"

There was a long silence. I couldn't tell what he was doing because I had the camera facing Ariana, but when I held it out in front of the both of us, I could see he stood stunned.

"Damn, baby, you are beautiful."

I thought I would never see the softer side of that nigga. I mean, he looked soft as a pillow, looking into the screen. I was actually shocked and amazed. I looked over at Tiny, and she looked just as shocked.

"Thank you, Daddy. "

"Put that muscle-head back on the phone, baby. Roman, where yo' punk-ass at?"

I faced the camera. "What up?"

"Yo, I know you had better not laid a finger on my daughter. She better still be a virgin, because if not, I swear I'm gon' track your ass down and kill you in cold blood. Now, listen, there has been a change of plans. I'm gon' send you this address, and I want you to punch it into your GPS system. Be here in three hours, and bring my baby with you."

***

"You're sure you reading that right?" I asked Tiny as she told me to make another left down a block so rundown it made the slums of Chicago look like the suburbs. It seemed like every house was boarded with those green boards they put on your windows when they raid your crib, or the DEA gotta step. We saw porches where it looked like 50+ dudes were standing in front of it just itching for a reason to do the most. Bums had more than a few garbage cans burning while they held their hands over the top of them, and on their faces were dirt and scowls so mean it looked like they hated everything in existence. We saw hookers that looked so rundown their hot clothes barely fit. They constantly coughed and spit up mucus, looked at our truck as if we were about to pull over and ask them for a date that might have ended with them stabbing one of us, or giving us a disease that would kill us eventually. The rain had stopped, and the sun peeked from behind the clouds. The signs told us we were in Detroit.

"Yeah, that's what the GPS say. That's what he told us to follow, so keep going," Tiny said, looking around nervously.

"Damn, I can't see why Jaheim would move out here. This place look like a zombie town. This is crazy."

I continued to roll, crossing over some tracks that had a dead dog laying in the middle of them with four other dogs eating from his body. I had never seen nothing like that before.

When our truck rolled over the tracks, they turned to look at us, and I could see the slain animal's blood all over their muzzles.

I took the road that led to the right of the tracks, and I started to smell odors so foul I wanted to throw up. To our left we saw a big plant with murky waters flowing into it and disappearing.

"Ew, what is that smell? That's horrible!" Ariana said, making the gag sound.

"I don't know, but I'm about to throw up that hotdog I ate. I'm not kidding." She gagged and lowered her window, and before she could say anything else, she was purging her guts along the side of the truck.

I swallowed and tried to get ahold of myself, but the smell was putrid. It made it hard to breathe. I started to cough, and my nose ran full of snot. "This must be some kind of sewer system."

I drove all the way up to the plant and parked the truck in front of the big, bricked building. There was a bright light that shined down, illuminating our car. It was so bright I was starting to get dizzy, and then all at once it shut off and the entire area went pitch black.

"Holy crap, what the hell is going on?" Ariana said, reaching over the seat and placing her arm around Tiny.

My phone vibrated. I activated it, and Jaheim's face popped on. "Welcome to the slums, muthafucka!"

As soon as he said this, we heard the sounds of what seemed to be motorcycles in the distance. A minute later, our car was surrounded by Jaheim and his masked goons.

Chapter 20

Tiny

They snatched us out of the truck and placed what seemed to be black pillowcases over our heads. The next thing I knew, we were in some kind of a dungeon, and the air was so cold I could not stop my knees from knocking into each other. I was freezing and scared out of my mind. When the pillowcases were pulled off of our heads, Jaheim stood in front of us with a huge machete in his hands. He had us sitting in metal chairs beside one another. I was shaking so bad my chair was rattling. I didn't know what this fool was up to, and I didn't know where I was. I was super terrified. How in the hell had I managed to survive 17 years in prison only to get out and find myself in a position like this? I had still not seen Alexis, and that was giving me a cause for concern.

"Now, ain't this a bitch, Zivial? I'm so happy to see you that I feel like screaming. What up, bitch?" He walked up to me and grabbed my hair and yanked my head forward. "It's been a long time coming, and Lord knows I been waiting for this. This is like a dream that's coming true. This shit is beautiful." He placed the machete to my neck. "I should cut your muthafuckin' head off right now and save me some time later."

"Daddy, no!" Ariana screamed.

He stepped to the side and stood in front of her. "What's the matter, baby? You don't want me to kill this bitch?"

"No, please don't." She had tears in her eyes. "Please don't kill anybody. I'm begging you."

He knelt down and rubbed his thumb over her cheek. "Okay, baby, I won't kill her right now, but I can't promise you it won't happen later. We'll just have to see where the cards fall, okay?"

She wiped her tears away and nodded. I could see she was shaking just as bad as I was. She looked as if she wanted to run away. When he rubbed her cheek, she'd closed her eyes as if she were repulsed by him.

"So, you're my little girl, huh? Don't you know I'm about to spoil you like crazy?" He kissed her on the forehead. "I been trying to find you ever since you were born, but this bitch over here kept you hidden from me. That's why I took her daughter away, to show her what it feels like." He pointed his machete at me. "This bitch been jealous ever since your mother came into the picture. It was her fault your mother started using, anyway. She put her on that shit, and she went out and bought it for her when she was trying to get herself together. We both were, but this bitch knew she was pregnant with you, so she decided to make things as tough as possible for your mother by playing on her mental defects. She mentally manipulated her on every single level until she packed that poison into her body so much she went crazy and killed herself. All of this came out of her jealousy." He spit on the concrete by my feet. "Admit it, bitch!"

I started to shake. Every single thing he'd told her was a flat-out lie. I mean, every piece of it was false. Me and Ariana's biological mother were friends that worked under Jaheim. He was the one that got her hooked on drugs, and he was the one that had mentally manipulated her on every level. I, on the other hand, did everything I could to shield her, and to protect her from him, but she became too addicted to the lifestyle and the dreams he had sold her. There was nothing I could do once she was all the way mentally gone and physically dependent on his drugs.

"Admit it, bitch. I ain't gon' tell you again!" he growled.

"No, it's not true. Amber was my friend. I would have never hurt her. I tried to save her because I loved her, and I have loved that child since day one."

"You lying bitch!" he backhanded me so fast I flew out of the seat and onto my face. He picked me up by the hair and slammed my face into the ground, knocking me out cold.

When I awoke, Ariana was holding a gun to Alexis' head while Jaheim held her by the neck. "Kill, this bitch, baby. Kill her like Tiny killed your mother. They don't love you like I do. You're my little girl, and I'll do anything for you. They brought you here to die."

Ariana had tears rolling down her cheeks. "Please, Daddy, don't tell me that. Don't tell me they brought me here to die, please." She tightened her grip on the handle of the gun.

Alexis sat in the chair, looking as if she were about to pass out. Her face was beaten and bloodied. She kept falling forward, and Jaheim would slam her back in the chair with his hand firm around her neck.

"Kill me, I don't care. I'm tired, anyway." She whispered with her eyes rolling into the back of her head.

"Fuck that, Jaheim. You wanted 500 thousand and your daughter, and that's what we brought to you. Now, let us go, man. This shit ain't right!" Roman hollered with the pillowcase still over his head.

Jaheim ripped it off. "You know what? I hate niggas. I really don't like the male species at all. One thing is for sure, that yo' punk-ass is dead. You and this other muthafucka back here."

He snapped his fingers and signaled. Seconds later, another man was thrown on the floor next to me with a black pillowcase over his head. He squirmed on the floor until Jaheim
kicked him in the stomach, flipping him on his back, and then put his boot over his neck and pressed down. "You're dead, too, fuck-nigga!" He lifted the machete over his head, ready to come down over the man's neck.

There was a loud boom, and then we heard a series of gunfire. It sounded like an army movie, except this was real life, and we could actually die.

Jaheim dived to the floor and came up with a gun, looking into the mist. More gunfire ensued. His men ran in the direction of where I was guessing we came in with assault rifles in their hands. Before they could make it all the way there, we saw about four vans roll into the cave-like dungeon, and out of them came about thirty armed men with assault rifles. They wasted no time firing in our direction and chopping his henchmen up.

I willed myself to get to Alexis, where I pulled her to the floor and covered her body with mine. I closed my eyes and said a prayer in my head. *Lord, please protect us, and do not let the Devil's bullets pierce our fleshy bodies. We need your protection, and your undeserved kindness.*

I squeezed my eyes tighter and told Alexis it was going to be alright. I heard more and more gunfire, and the smell was enough to make me sick. It must have gone on for a full ten minutes until slowly it died down.

I did not open my eyes until I felt somebody rubbing my back and telling me it was okay now to get up. I opened them to see King extending a hand to me. He helped me up, and I pulled Alexis along with me. She nearly fell back over, but I held onto her for dear life.

"Let's get her to a hospital," King said, helping me carry her.

As I looked around, I saw bodies all over the place. It looked like there had been a massacre. I looked around for Jaheim and saw him in the middle of the dungeon with so many bullet holes in him he looked like Swiss cheese, and as sinister as it was, all I could do was smile.

I saw Ariana being helped into the van alongside Roman, and that made me happy. I felt everything was finally going to fall into place, but little did I know it was just the beginning, and this story was far from over.

To Be Continued...
Loyal to the Game 4: Ariana's Revenge
Coming Soon

A Word to You Queens

My sisters, the first rule in life is to love yourself, or you leave no room for anyone else to be able to do so. You must understand you are precious and God created you with a distinct vision in mind. Every part of you was made and crafted for a specific purpose.

When you look into the mirror, you should see nothing other than beauty. Your beauty! You are one of a kind, and there is none like you. You *cannot* and will not ever be duplicated. Embrace your treasures and seek the blessings God has in store for you. You were created to be the Queen of something. All you have to do is take the time to find out exactly what that is.

It took me a long time to be able to embrace who I am. I experienced many heartbreaks. I spent many nights crying alone, trying to figure out exactly who I was and what my purpose was for being placed here on this earth. Sometimes it takes a person losing something in order to gain themselves.

Today, I can honestly say I am still working on fully discovering myself. I am struggling to be able to unconditionally love me. It's hard work, and it begins deep within the soul.

Thank you for reading *Loyal to the Game*. Please look for many other novels by me. I am here to stay, and through these pages I have found I am able to be me, and that this is the most beautiful part of myself I can share with the world.

Take brick by brick, and you will find it is not a difficult task building your own foundation. Place your faith in Him and all your dreams will come true.

Love yourselves, and God Bless!

T.J.

Message from the author...

Love yourself, Li'l Mama, because the world is designed to hate you.
Seek to find guidance, because those that walk beside your presence will mentally, emotionally, and physically rape you,
And there is no place to escape to
Other than the inner you,
The inner you that must be strong and impenetrable.
You will never find the strength and worth that transcends the outer you. Even if the world says that you're beautiful,
You won't believe it!
Believe in you and become obsessed with the fact that you ARE a WOMAN.
And nothing can be more precious than that –
NOTHING!

–Jelissa

Stay Connected with Us!

Text **LOCKDOWN** to 22828 to stay up-to-date with new releases, sneak peaks, contests and more...

Thank you!

Coming Soon from Lock Down Publications/Ca$h Presents

BOW DOWN TO MY GANGSTA

By **Ca$h & Jamaica**

TORN BETWEEN TWO

By **Coffee**

BLOOD OF A BOSS **IV**

By **Askari**

BRIDE OF A HUSTLA **III**

THE FETTI GIRLS **II**

By **Destiny Skai**

WHEN A GOOD GIRL GOES BAD **II**

By **Adrienne**

LOVE & CHASIN' PAPER **II**

By **Qay Crockett**

THE HEART OF A GANGSTA **II**

By **Jerry Jackson**

TO DIE IN VAIN **II**

By **ASAD**

LOYAL TO THE GAME **III**

By **TJ & Jelissa**

A DOPEBOY'S PRAYER **II**

By **Eddie "Wolf" Lee**
A HUSTLER'S DECEIT **III**
THE BOSS MAN'S DAUGHTERS **III**
BAE BELONGS TO ME **II**
By **Aryanna**

<u>**Available Now**</u>
(CLICK TO PURCHASE)
<u>RESTRAINING ORDER **I & II**</u>
By **CA$H & Coffee**
<u>LOVE KNOWS NO BOUNDARIES **I II & III**</u>
By **Coffee**
<u>LAY IT DOWN **I & II**</u>
<u>LAST OF A DYING BREED</u>
By **Jamaica**
<u>LOYAL TO THE GAME</u>
<u>LOYAL TO THE GAME II</u>
By **TJ & Jelissa**
<u>PUSH IT TO THE LIMIT</u>
By **Bre' Hayes**
<u>BLOOD OF A BOSS **I II & III**</u>
By **Askari**

THE STREETS BLEED MURDER **I, II & III**

THE HEART OF A GANGSTA

By **Jerry Jackson**

CUM FOR ME

CUM FOR ME 2

CUM FOR ME 3

An **LDP Erotica Collaboration**

BRIDE OF A HUSTLA **I & II**

By **Destiny Skai**

WHEN A GOOD GIRL GOES BAD

By **Adrienne**

A GANGSTER'S REVENGE **I II III & IV**

THE BOSS MAN'S DAUGHTERS

THE BOSS MAN'S DAUGHTERS II

A SAVAGE LOVE **I & II**

BAE BELONGS TO ME

A HUSTLER'S DECEIT I, II

By **Aryanna**

A KINGPIN'S AMBITON

By **Ambitious**

A DOPEBOY'S PRAYER

By **Eddie "Wolf" Lee**

WHAT ABOUT US **I & II**

NEVER LOVE AGAIN

THUG ADDICTION

By **Kim Kaye**

THE KING CARTEL **I, II & III**

By **Frank Gresham**

THESE NIGGAS AIN'T LOYAL **I, II & III**

By **Nikki Tee**

GANGSTA SHYT **I II &III**

By **CATO**

THE ULTIMATE BETRAYAL

By **Phoenix**

DON'T FU#K WITH MY HEART **I & II**

By **Linnea**

BOSS'N UP **I & II**

By **Royal Nicole**

I LOVE YOU TO DEATH

By Destiny J

I RIDE FOR MY HITTA

I STILL RIDE FOR MY HITTA

By **Misty Holt**

LOVE & CHASIN' PAPER

By **Qay Crockett**

<u>TO DIE IN VAIN</u>

By **ASAD**

<u>BOOKS BY LDP'S CEO, CA$H</u>

(CLICK TO PURCHASE)

<u>TRUST IN NO MAN</u>

<u>TRUST IN NO MAN 2</u>

<u>TRUST IN NO MAN 3</u>

<u>BONDED BY BLOOD</u>

<u>SHORTY GOT A THUG</u>

<u>THUGS CRY</u>

<u>THUGS CRY 2</u>

<u>THUGS CRY 3</u>

<u>TRUST NO BITCH</u>

<u>TRUST NO BITCH 2</u>

<u>TRUST NO BITCH 3</u>

<u>TIL MY CASKET DROPS</u>

<u>RESTRAINING ORDER</u>

<u>RESTRAINING ORDER 2</u>

<u>IN LOVE WITH A CONVICT</u>

<u>Coming Soon</u>

BONDED BY BLOOD 2

BOW DOWN TO MY GANGSTA

Loyal to the Game 3